A FATAL MISTAKE...

"Draw, Ramsey," Conley challenged.

"Forget it," said Matt. He walked down to the hitching rail and reached for the reins of his black.

Conley pulled his revolver out of its holster and leveled the barrel at Matt's back. He thumbed back the hammer.

Matt threw himself backward into the dirt, and Conley's bullet went high, kicking up dust. The stallion snorted and danced back into the street.

Matt's Colt was out and he pulled the trigger. The bullet crushed Conley's sternum and slammed him up against the front wall of the Spalding House.

He stood there for an instant, an expression of disbelief on his face, his right arm still extended in front of him but the fingers going limp, the gun barrel pointing at the ground just in front of him. Then the revolver slipped from them and fell to the sidewalk. The expression went blank, and the head fell back. Then the body dropped to its knees, and slowly pitched forward. . . .

THE DEADLY STRANGER

WILL McLENNAN

JOVE BOOKS, NEW YORK

THE DEADLY STRANGER

A Jove Book/published by arrangement with
the author

PRINTING HISTORY
Jove edition/September 1990

ISBN: 0-515-10400-0

Jove Books are published by The Berkley Publishing Group,
200 Madison Avenue, New York, New York 10016.
The name "JOVE" and the "J" logo
are trademarks belonging to Jove Publications, Inc.

PRINTED IN THE UNITED STATES OF AMERICA

10 9 8 7 6 5 4 3 2 1

THE DEADLY STRANGER

CHAPTER

★ 1 ★

Clarence Dodd was broke. He couldn't exactly say that he was out of a job, because he had never really had a job in his twenty-one years. He had lived off of his father's wealth in Boston and enjoyed the good life, drinking, gambling, and chasing women. All that had finally come to an end, though, when he had gone too far, even for old Horace Dodd. He had gambled big and lost big, and he had given his marker to the winner. Then the winner and his friends, all unsavory types, had paid old Horace a visit. Horace had made good on the marker, but a major confrontation between father and son had followed. They had almost come to blows, and Clarence had ended it by storming out of the house and vowing never to return. He had tried to get into a poker game on credit and been thrown out. He didn't know where to turn. He was beginning to feel desperate.

He was hungry and alone, and he had no place to stay. He could probably have gone back to his father and begged and whined his way back in, but he had decided that he would not do that. Not this time. He had discovered, to his own surprise, that he did have some pride. No. He would not go crawling back home to grovel at the feet of Horace Dodd. It was getting late and places were starting to close. Not that it mattered much. With no money to spend, he couldn't have made use of them open anyway. He passed a pawn shop with its front gate pulled together and padlocked, and an idea came into his head and he made a quick decision.

He hurried around the corner and went down the alley to find the back of the pawn shop. It had a back door, but that, too, was securely locked. Clarence shot quick glances up and down the alley. He was alone. There was a window in the shop's back door, and Clarence pulled his handkerchief out of his pocket and wrapped it around his right hand. He looked again to his right and his left, and still he saw no one in the alley. He drove his fist through the window glass just at the pane's lower right-hand corner. Then he flattened himself against the wall, terrified that the noise of the shattering glass had drawn some attention. He waited, his heart pounding, drawing short and shallow breaths, and he watched. No one came. Clarence reached back through the broken glass and found the latch on the inside of the door. Soon he was inside. It was dark in the shop, darker even than the alley outside. God, he thought, what now? Slowly his eyes began to adjust, and he could make out where shelves and counters and cases stood. He started to look for the cash register. Once he bumped into a glass case, and he thought that the noise it made had been heard up and down the street outside. He stood still for a moment, then renewed his search.

He found the cash register and fumbled with it for a while. He pulled the handle and hit keys. He struck the damnable machine with his fist. At last he hit the right key and pulled the handle and the drawer flew open, almost frightening him. There were a few bills and some small change in the drawer, and he grabbed it all and stuffed it into his pockets. Damn, he thought. He had expected more. The shifty bastard of a pawnbroker must take his money out at night, take it home or put it in a bank. There should have been more. He turned to leave the shop and his eyes lit on a glass case filled with handguns. He didn't know anything about guns, but he felt that he should have something besides pocket change for his labors. A variety of guns were displayed in the case, and he didn't know one from another, but there was one in a box with a box of bullets there, too. The bullets must fit the gun. He took out the box of bullets and dropped it in his right-hand jacket pocket. Then he took the pistol and tucked it into the waistband of his trousers. He pulled his jacket front together and buttoned it.

It had taken longer to get served and to eat his meal than Tod Stover had anticipated, and he was afraid that he would be late for the train. He had purchased a ticket for the first leg of his journey west, and he would purchase the other half on down the line. Someone had told him that it would be cheaper that way. He didn't know, but he had decided to try it and find out. It couldn't hurt anything. But the meal had taken too long, and now he had only a few minutes to reach the depot in time. The man had told him that if he missed the train he would be out of luck—and out of the money he had spent on the ticket. "No refunds," he had said. He told himself that he should have left the meal half finished. He had thought about that while he was eating, but he had not done it. Now as he rushed along the sidewalks, he was sorry that he had not heeded his own advice. He had enough money on him to buy another ticket, but he hated the thought of wasting the first ticket and of having to wait for another train. He had a mission out West, a mission to fulfill his father's dying wish, and he intended to get it done and to get it done without wasting any time. His bag was already at the station, probably already loaded on the train. He felt for the money belt around his waist. It was secure. He reached inside his coat and felt the letter there in the inside pocket. Everything was in order, if only he could make the depot on time. He turned down a sidestreet and cut down the alley. It would be quicker.

Clarence Dodd stepped out into the alley and pulled the door closed behind him. He looked to his right and saw no one. He turned to look to his left, and Tod Stover almost ran into him there in the dark. Tod stopped. Both men shouted in surprise and fright. Clarence, thinking he had been caught in the act, swung a wild right at Tod's head. Tod just managed to duck and avoid the blow, which knocked the bowler off his head. He spread his arms, lowered his head, and rushed forward, ramming his head into Clarence's sternum and knocking the wind out of him. His arms encircled Clarence's upper body, pinning Clarence's arms to his sides, and the forward momentum carried both men to the ground. Clarence struggled ineffectively to get free and to get his breath back. Tod, on top and at least theoretically in control, tried to figure out what to do next. In order to strike his opponent, he would have to release his grip. That would allow the other fellow to strike at him, too. While he was trying to make up his mind, Clarence bit his ear, and he screamed in pain, surprise, and indignation. He also released his grip and sat up, straddling Clarence's waist, and swung a right that caught Clarence on the side of the head. Clarence howled in pain and anger and flailed wildly with both arms and legs. Tod held his arms up in front of his face in an attempt to fend off the blows for a few seconds, then he stood up quickly and stepped back a few steps, striking a prizefighter's posture.

"Come on," he said. "Come on, you ear-biter, you."

As Clarence turned to one side to get to his feet, he saw a fist-sized rock lying there beside him. He grasped it firmly in his right hand, stood up, and swung with all his might. The rock bashed into the left side of Tod's head, and Tod's face went blank. His knees buckled, and he crumpled into a little pile there in the alley.

"My God!" said Clarence. "I've killed the son of a bitch! Oh, no."

He turned to run. Then he had a second thought. He knelt beside the lifeless form there in the alley and rolled it over on its back. He felt the pockets of the jacket. He found a piece of paper in the inside coat pocket, and he pulled that out and stuffed it into his own pocket. In an outside pocket he found a ticket. He would look at that in the light and see what he had. He found a few bills and some change in other pockets, and he added this to what he had stolen in the pawn shop. Then he ran. Out on the street under the light of a lamppost, he looked at the ticket. It was a train ticket, going west, in about four minutes. It didn't take Clarence long to make up his mind. He needed to get out of the city before the body was discovered. He had no place to go in Boston anyhow. He ran to the depot and caught the train, just in time.

Tod Stover groaned and rolled over onto his stomach. His head hurt like a fury. He put a hand to his head and felt the sticky blood in his matted hair. The touch hurt, and again he groaned out loud. He pushed himself up to his knees and then sat up straight. He allowed his head to fall back, and he looked up into the dark sky. A long, low wail escaped his lips. His head hurt. He did not know where he was. He was lost and alone, and slowly the worst of it dawned on his consciousness! He did not know who he was.

CHAPTER

★ 2 ★

Matt Ramsey rode north and a little west. He had no particular destination in mind, no real goals. He was just leaving Texas and the memories it held for him. He knew that he could never erase from his mind the images of violence in his war-torn home, or the miseries and corruption of postwar reconstruction in the South, but he had a feeling that the farther away from Texas he could take himself, the fainter the memories might become. He hoped that the images would grow vague and dim with distance. But the trail was a long and lonely one, and there was nothing to do except move, nothing with which to occupy one's mind and energies except bare survival, and neither of these things put much strain on Matt Ramsey. So he thought about the past. He recalled the violence and the bloodshed. He mourned for the victims of that time, and he harbored a deep

7

sense of guilt; he nurtured remorse for the active part he himself had played in those destructive events.

He rode north and a little west. It would be colder up there, and he would find a different kind of people. The war and reconstruction had not touched that country with the same fury with which they had ravaged his home. Perhaps it would deaden the pain. Perhaps. As he rode on, he thought about his brothers. Each was dealing with the pangs of the past in his own way. Amos had stayed home with his family, where he was working the old family farm. Farming was hard work, Matt knew. Maybe it took up all of Amos's time and energy and, therefore, kept him from dwelling on the past. That and the family. Raising a family was a big job, too. So Amos had the farm and his family. Luke had married, too, but he and his new wife didn't have any children yet—not that Matt knew about—and they had left home. Luke was raising horses on the Trinity River. Probably soon be raising kids there too, Matt thought. And Kyle, as far as Matt knew, was still in the Colorado gold fields. He wondered if his brother had struck it rich yet. The thought made him smile as he rode along. Kyle a rich man. He tried to picture Kyle in a frock coat, a vest, and striped trousers. Black, shiny button shoes and spats. A top hat and a walking stick. He chuckled out loud at the image he had conjured up in his mind. He hoped that Kyle would strike it rich; he'd like to see him like that. Yes, indeed. And then there was Bucky. Little Bucky. He had gone back to Texas, but beyond that, Matt had no idea. Knowing his youngest brother's inclinations, though, Matt figured that he was probably punching cows somewhere.

It was sad to think what this country did to families. A family ought to stay together. In Matt's mind, there wasn't anything more important than family. Without family, nothing else really mattered. What else was worth fighting and dying for? For that matter, what else was worth living for? Family was everything, yet this country tore families apart and sent them off in all different directions. Matt didn't know about the East—and he didn't want to know—but he knew the West. It was a hard and cold country, and it didn't care a damn about a man. It could freeze him or burn him to death. It could get him lost and make him crazy, but the worst thing it did, in the mind of Matt Ramsey, was rip apart families. God damn this country, he said to himself as he rode, but even as he said it, he knew that he would trade it for no other.

A train whistle sounded in the distance. The big black stallion nickered and balked slightly at the sudden, unexpected noise, and Matt, too, was shocked out of his reverie. For an instant, he didn't know what it was. A railroad—anything that smacked even slightly of civilization—was the farthest thing from his mind. He settled the black horse down.

"Train coming," he said. He stretched his neck and looked off in the distance, trying to figure where the tracks might be. He decided that they would probably be running directly across his path down below the next rise. He touched his spurs to the stallion's flanks, just enough to get the message across, and began to lope toward the rise. He wasn't sure why he wanted to see the train. Just because it was there, he guessed. He hadn't really seen all that many trains in his life, and he still felt a little of that thrill, the feeling of little boys who ran to the tracks to watch the train come in. He would ride up ahead and watch the train go by, then he would follow the tracks. They would lead him to a town. He didn't know what the town would be, and he didn't really care. It would be a place where he could get a pre-pared meal and a drink of whiskey and a bed for the night. The black would get some oats and a stall and a much-needed rest.

He topped the rise and saw the train coming from the east. The tracks, as he had guessed, were down below, about a hundred yards or so. The train came closer, and Matt took off his dusty hat and waved it in the air over his head. An arm came out of the sleek black engine and waved back, and the whistle sounded again. The engineer had seen him and waved back. The black stallion pranced under him, and Matt grinned. There had been a civilized ex-change of greetings out on the wide open prairie, and soon the train would be out of sight and there would be no evidence of its passing. Or so Matt Ramsey thought.

But as he watched it recede toward the west, he saw a strange thing. A body came flying out of a boxcar to hit and bounce and roll there on the south side of the tracks.

"Damn," said Matt, and again he spurred the stal-lion, this time with more urgency. He was about halfway to the spot where the body had landed when he saw the man struggling to his feet. At least he's not killed, Matt thought. Not even hurt bad, it seems. He rode on up to the man and reined in the stallion.

"You all right, mister?" he said.

Clarence Dodd was slapping dust off his trousers. He looked up at Matt Ramsey on the big black stallion.

"Yeah," he said. "I think so. Did you see that?"

Matt pointed back to the rise behind him.

"I was sitting right up there. Just waved at the engineer, and he tooted back at me."

"Well," said Clarence, "I don't know just how to feel about that. A part of me says that I wish there had been no witnesses to my rather inglorious debarkation from that—iron horse. It's damned embarrassing. Another part tells me to be glad I'm not out here alone. This is pretty desolate-looking country."

"It's more than desolate *looking*," said Matt. "I can guarantee that. You sure you ain't got no broken bones? Tromp around a bit and make sure."

Clarence walked around in a circle and waved his arms.

"Everything seems to be okay," he said. He stretched a hand up toward Matt. "By the way, I'm Tod Stover."

"Matt Ramsey," said Matt, taking the hand. "Uh, how come they tossed you off like that?"

"Well," said Clarence, "I had a ticket that took me only as far as the last stopping-off place, but I wasn't ready to get off. I couldn't afford the price of a ticket on down the road, so I just sort of . . . hid out. For a while at least."

"I see," said Matt. He pointed to the ground behind Clarence. "That your Galand and Sommerville there?"

"What?"

"That funny little pistol there on the ground. Bullets scattered around. That's a Galand and Sommerville .450 self-extracting revolver, ain't it?"

"Oh," said Clarence. "Oh, that. Yeah. It's mine."

He bent to pick it up, and Matt's right hand automatically went to the butt of his Colt. Clarence saw the movement and hesitated. He reached slowly for the barrel of the .450.

"It's not loaded," he said. "See?"

He handed the pistol to Matt. Then he started picking up bullets and dropping them into his coat pocket. Matt turned the funny-looking weapon over in his hands. He took it in his right hand and held it out as if to shoot, testing its heft. He pulled back the hammer, then pulled the trigger and let the hammer click.

"I guess it'd do in a pinch," he said. "Only one thing."

"What's that?" said Clarence.

"Like you said: It ain't loaded. Unloaded gun ain't worth a damn."

He tossed the pistol back to Clarence, who caught it with both hands against his stomach.

"I guess you're right. I'd better load it. I really don't know much about guns. I just thought, coming west, I might need one. I bought it in Boston."

Matt swung down out of the saddle and let the reins trail in the dirt. He bent down on one knee to help Clarence pick up the scattered bullets.

"If you was riding hid," he said, "you're probably

hungry. I'm fixing to make a camp just up ahead. You're welcome to join me."

"Thanks," said Clarence. "That's the best offer I've had all day."

They finished eating the trail meal that Matt had prepared, and they were having another cup of coffee. It was still early evening. The sun was low in the sky, but it was not yet getting dark.

"What's the name of that town you were headed for?" asked Matt.

"Lane Rock," said Clarence. "It's somewhere along those tracks. That's about all I know."

"You never been there before?"

"Well, uh, yeah," said Clarence, "but I was just a kid."

"You got a reason for going back there?" asked Matt.

"Well," said Clarence, "not really. I don't have a job. Don't really have anything to hold me anywhere. My dad was pretty important back in Lane Rock a few years ago. Seems like it might be a good place for me to get a start."

"I don't mean to be prying," said Matt. "Just making conversation. If I ask too many questions, just tell me."

"Oh, that's all right. I've got no secrets, and you've done me a real great favor. I'd rather talk than just sit here anyway."

Matt moved over to the small fire and checked the coffee pot.

"There's still some here," he said. "Want a refill?"

"Yeah. Thanks."

Matt refilled the cups, then settled back down.

"Lane Rock," he said. "I ain't never been there. You don't know how far it is?"

"No," said Clarence, "I'm afraid not."

Matt stood up and looked west down the long line of railroad tracks. Aside from the rise to the south of the tracks on which they were camped, the country was flat. Mountains could be seen way off in the distance.

"Well, Tod, old buddy," he said, "I tell you what. However far it is, it's too damn far to walk. I can see that from here."

"I don't have a whole lot of choice," said Clarence.

"Well, I'm fixing to give you one. I was just thinking to myself, just before I seen you flying through the air, that it was about time I visited myself a town. Had a bath and a drink. Slept in a bed. Just for a change. Lane Rock sounds like the nearest town to me. Guess I'll be heading for it. Might be another two, three days' ride anyhow, and I could use some company. Keep me from thinking too much."

Matt had a sudden flashback of the war and its aftermath in Texas, and he thought again of his brothers and wondered how they were doing. Yes, he needed some company just now for distraction.

"You mean," said Clarence, "we could travel along together?"

"That's my suggestion."

"But you've only got one horse."

"That old black stallion is one strong son of a bitch," said Matt. "He can carry double if he has to. Better yet, one of us can ride while the other walks. Take turns. We'll make it all right."

"Well, thanks," said Clarence. "Thanks, Matt. Shoot, when they threw me off that train, I thought I'd hit bottom. I thought my luck was all played out. I was sure wrong. I couldn't have had a better stroke of luck than when you came riding up on me."

"Like I said," said Matt, "I'm glad for the company. Say, I've got an idea. How would you like to learn to use that funny little English revolver you bought in Boston?"

"Yeah. Yeah, I'd like to do that."

"Well, haul it out and load it up," said Matt, and he went on a search of the surrounding ground for fist-sized rocks. Clarence pulled the revolver out and fumbled in his coat pocket for bullets. In a couple of minutes he had figured out how to load the weapon. He watched as Matt lined up rocks at a distance of twenty-five or so paces, and he thought happily that his luck had indeed changed for the better. When his father had thrown him out of the house back in Boston, Clarence had not known where he would go or what he would do. Then he had made a bumbling attempt at robbery. There had not been enough money in the cash register at the pawn shop to make the effort worthwhile, and on escaping from the pawn shop, he had been spotted. He had fought with the man in the alley, Tod Stover, and he had beaten him. He had gotten a few more dollars off of Stover, but most important, he had gotten the train ticket and the letter. Stover was obviously important in Lane Rock. If he went into Lane Rock posing as Stover, he would receive good treatment. There was bound to be a way to turn some profit by this whole thing. There was only one sour note in the whole symphony, and that was the killing of Stover. Clarence felt badly about that. He hadn't intended to kill anyone. It had just happened. He tried not to think about it. It was over and done, and the thing for Clarence to do now was to take whatever advantage he could of the situation he found himself in. Well, he resolved that he would make the most of it.

And not the least of this recent run of luck was running into Matt Ramsey. Clarence liked Ramsey, but even more important, Ramsey seemed like a man who could handle himself in just about any situation that might arise. He would be a good man to be able to call a friend. This was a strange country to Clarence, and he needed the help and guidance of a man like Ramsey. Clarence would not have believed it beforehand, but on reflection, he thought that getting thrown off the train was one of the best things that had happened to him. It had thrown him right into the path of Matt Ramsey.

"Tod," said Matt.

Clarence jumped up to his feet. "Yeah?"

"You got that thing loaded?"

"Yeah. All loaded up."

"Bring it over here."

Clarence walked over to Matt, the Galand and Sommerville in his right hand.

"Let me see that thing," said Matt.

Clarence handed the revolver to Matt, who checked the load.

"This is all right for now," he said, "but let me tell you something."

"Okay."

"How you been carrying this thing?"

He handed the revolver back to Clarence, and Clarence tucked it into the waistband of his trousers.

"Like this," he said.

"When you load a revolver up full," said Matt, "that means that your hammer is resting on a loaded chamber. If something was to happen to cause that thing to go off, you can see what you might lose. If it was me, I'd leave one chamber empty and let the hammer rest on that one."

"I see what you mean," said Clarence, slowly withdrawing the revolver from his waistband. "I'll remember that."

Matt pulled out his Colt and aimed at the rock on the far right of the lineup he had made. He squeezed the trigger, and Clarence flinched at the unexpected loudness of the blast. The rock hopped up a few inches off the ground and fell back to earth.

"Your shot," said Matt.

Clarence stuck his strange-looking revolver out at arm's length and jerked the trigger. The shot went high and wide.

"Damn," he said.

"That's all right," said Matt. "First thing: Don't jerk the trigger. Squeeze it real easy. When you jerk it, you pull up. Makes you shoot high. Let me see it."

Clarence handed the revolver to Matt, and Matt held it out and fired. His first shot went high. He lowered the barrel just a tad and fired again. The second shot hit the rock. He handed the gun back to Clarence.

"It shoots just a bit high," he said. "Aim just a little below what you want to hit. Now, try it again. Aim low and squeeze."

Clarence took aim and squeezed the trigger. His shot was a little short.

"That was too low," said Matt. "Try again. You'll get it figured out."

Clarence took aim again. He fired and hit his mark.

"I got it!" he shouted. "I got it!"

Tod Stover wandered aimlessly the streets of Boston. Nothing seemed familiar. His mind was not exactly a blank. It was full of questions. Where am I? What is this place? Where should I be? Shouldn't I be someplace? Aren't there places where people belong? All of these people on the street—they seem to be going places. They're not aimless, the way I am. *I. I?* Who am I? He looked into the faces of the people he passed on the street, hoping to see something, someone familiar, hoping for some clue to something. He studied the street itself, the storefronts. He had to have come from somewhere. Someone somewhere had to know him. He couldn't have just been dropped into this neighborhood. There must be a reason he was there. There must be. He kept searching.

Up ahead a man stood on the street corner selling newspapers. Tod walked straight up to the man and stared him in the eyes.

"Here now," said the man. "What's the matter?"

Tod didn't answer. He just kept staring. He had

no idea what a frightening aspect he carried. He was ordinarily a handsome young man, but now blood was caked on the side of his head. His hair was matted and mussed, and his clothes were rumpled from the fight and from lying for hours in the alley. His expression was distracted.

"Do you want a paper?" asked the man.

"Do you know me?" asked Tod.

"What?"

"Do you know who I am?"

"Are you crazy?"

"I don't know," said Tod. "I don't know who I am. I'm lost."

"You're hurt," said the newspaperman. "Just take it easy. You need a copper. That's what you need. Just hold on."

He looked frantically up and down the street. About a block down the street a man in a blue uniform, his hands folded behind his back, was strolling away from them. The newspaperman waved his arms wildly over his head.

"Liam," he shouted. "Hey, Sergeant O'Casey! Down here. Help! Police!"

Matt Ramsey walked along beside the big black stallion, the reins in his hands. Clarence Dodd sat in the saddle. Even though Matt liked the young man he knew as Tod Stover, he couldn't bring himself to let another man ride his horse and hold the reins. He had to maintain control. A man could ride off and leave another man to die in this hard country. So he held the reins while Clarence rode.

"Those mountains seem as far away as they did when we started," said Clarence.

"No," said Matt, "we're getting closer. Let's take a breather here."

He stopped the stallion, and Clarence climbed down out of the saddle, feeling stiff and sore. Matt took the canteen off the saddle and offered Clarence a drink. Then he had one himself. He put the canteen back on the saddle and looked around. Spotting a large flat rock, he sat down on it and pulled some tobacco out of his pocket. He rolled himself a cigarette and handed the makings to Clarence. Clarence took them and fumbled with the paper and tobacco.

"Here," said Matt. He handed Clarence the cigarette he had already rolled and took back the makings.

"Now watch," he said, and he rolled another. Then he fished a match out of his shirt pocket and struck it. Cupping the flame in his palms, he held it for Clarence to light his cigarette, then lit his own and broke the match in half. The stallion pulled at some bunch grass as the two men sat and smoked. The sun was low in the western sky. Another day was almost done.

"How much farther, do you think?" asked Clarence.

"You forget," said Matt, "you're the one who told me there was a town out there."

"Oh, yeah," said Clarence. "That's right."

"But I think that when we top that next rise we'll see it."

"How do you figure that?"

"Judging from the mountains. The town's got to be between us and the mountains. I think we'll see it from that rise." He tossed the butt of his cigarette aside. "Let's go," he said.

CHAPTER

★ 3 ★

Lane Rock was a small, insignificant town at the foot of the mountains. A town that had grown up as a result of the mining boom of a few years before, it was barely hanging on since most of the nearby mines had played out. There were a few scattered houses, and a few stubborn miners continued to scratch out a living in the old mines up in the mountains that loomed over the town, but mostly Lane Rock was one street of businesses. About half of the buildings were empty, and the other half were occupied by businessmen who hung on by catering to the few remaining local residents and the one-time customers who disembarked from a westbound train when it made a rest stop. The railroad had saved the town.

All of this was evident to Matt Ramsey as he rode into Lane Rock on his black stallion, Clarence Dodd walking alongside.

"I don't know, Tod," said Matt. "This don't exactly look like the land of opportunity to me."

"Yeah," said Clarence, "well, you never know."

A livery stable stood off to Matt's right, on the north side of the street, the first building they came to.

"Might as well stop right here," said Matt. He swung down out of the saddle and led the black by the reins into the stable. No one was in sight. Clarence walked back out into the street and looked up and down for someone who might know something. Finally a man came trotting toward him at an angle from across the street.

"Howdy," said the man. "Can I help you?"

"My friend's inside with his horse," said Clarence, and he followed the man inside. Matt had already unsaddled the stallion and backed him into a stall.

"Howdy," said the man, "I'm Lester Wiggins."

"This your place?" asked Matt.

"Yes sir. I don't get many customers anymore, though. That's why I wasn't watching too close when you came in. Most strangers who come into Lane Rock anymore come on the train."

"I took the liberty of putting my horse up here," said Matt.

"That's fine."

"Take good care of him. I'll make it worth your while. Name's Matt Ramsey."

"You going to be in town long, Mr. Ramsey?" asked Wiggins.

"I don't know, Mr. Wiggins," said Matt. "I'm just stopping over for a rest. Take it a day at a time. Is that all right with you?"

"That's fine. Just fine." Wiggins turned to Clarence. "How about you, sir?" he asked.

"Oh, I think I'll stick around for a while," said Clarence.

"Good," said Wiggins. "Good. Not many folks move into Lane Rock these days. Folks mostly move out. Glad to have you. We could use some new blood in town. Oh, by the way, I'm on the town council here. Uh, I didn't catch your name."

"I guess that's because I didn't give it," said Clarence. "I'm Tod Stover."

"Well, I'm pleased to know you, Mr. Stover," said Wiggins, offering his hand first to Clarence, then to Matt. "Pleased to know you both. I guess you'll be wanting a place to stay."

"And get a bath," said Matt.

"Well, the Spalding House is just a couple of doors down and across the street. It's run by another town-council member, Granville Spalding, a good man. He don't rent out too many rooms anymore. Runs a saloon downstairs, but he'll be glad to set you up. You can get a bath there too, up in the room. Tell him I sent you over. I'd walk over with you, but I'd best look to your horse there first."

"That's fine," said Matt. "We'll find our way."

"Thanks, Mr. Wiggins," said Clarence.

Matt slung his saddle roll over his shoulder and pulled the Winchester from the saddle boot before heading out the door. Clarence followed him, and they headed for the Spalding House. The few people out on the street gave them curious looks as they passed by. Inside the Spalding House, a few customers sat around tables in the saloon, though no one was behind the counter on the hotel side of the big room. Matt walked to the counter anyway and tossed his saddle roll down, laying the rifle beside it. He leaned an elbow on the counter and looked over in the direction of the saloon. Clarence stood beside him, fidgeting slightly. Soon the man behind the bar in the saloon saw them and came running. He went around behind the counter.

"Hello," he said. "I'm Granville Spalding. What can I do for you?"

"Wiggins over at the stable said we could get a room here," said Matt. "And a bath."

"You sure can," said Spalding. He blew the dust off his hotel register and turned the book around for Matt to sign. "I don't get many guests in the hotel anymore. I have a couple of permanent residents, but no other guests. Just sign here. You each want a room? I mean, one room each?"

Clarence looked at the floor, obviously embarrassed.

"I'm afraid that I'm a little short," he said.

"You got a room with two beds in it?" asked Matt.

"Yes."

"Is that cheaper than two rooms?"

"Yes. A little."

"We'll take that," said Matt. He signed his name in the book.

"Uh, you too, sir," said Spalding. "Would you sign the book too?"

Clarence signed in as "Tod Stover" and spun the book back around to face Spalding. Spalding turned around and took a key off a hook on the wall behind him, thought again, and took another key. He handed one to Matt and the other to Clarence.

"Just at the top of the stairs," he said. "First door on your left. I'll have the bath ready in just a few minutes. Uh, how long will you gentlemen be with us?"

"I don't know," said Matt. "Does it matter?"

"No. No. Not a bit. I'll get that bath ready now."

Tod Stover lay in a hospital bed. He had been washed and checked over thoroughly for injuries, and his head was bandaged where he had been hit by Clarence Dodd with the rock. Still he was confused. A doctor stood on one side of the bed, a police detective on the other. Tod looked around the room. He looked from the doctor to the policeman. None of it meant anything to him.

"Your name is Tod Stover," said the detective. "Tod Stover. Does that sound familiar?"

"No," said Tod. "Well, maybe. A little bit. Tod Stover . . . Tod. I don't know."

"Well, we found your identification in your wallet. That's your name—Tod Stover. You live right here in Boston. Or at least you did. We checked your address. The one on your identification card. You lived there with your father, Mr. Chad Stover, up until last month, when he died."

"My father?" said Tod.

"Yes."

"My father died?"

"Yes. Do you remember your father?"

"No. I don't know."

"Well, according to your landlord, when your father died, you took care of the funeral, sold all your belongings, and moved out of the apartment. We have no new address for you. Your landlord, Mr. Draper... Do you know Mr. Draper?"

"No. I can't remember. I don't know."

"Well," continued the detective, "Mr. Draper, your landlord, said that you gave no forwarding address. You told him that you would be leaving Boston. You said that you were going west. To a place called Lane Rock."

"Lane Rock," repeated Tod.

"Does any of that mean anything to you?" asked the policeman.

"No," said Tod. "I just don't know. I'm sorry. I don't know."

"That's all right, Tod," said the doctor. "We're just trying to help you. Knowing all this, maybe you'll start to remember before long."

"You have a considerable amount of money," said the detective. "It was in a money belt around your waist. Whoever attacked you—if he was out to rob you—didn't find the money belt. Do you know if you had anything else? Anything he might have stolen from you?"

Tod reached up with his right hand and felt his left breast.

"A letter," he said. "I had a letter. Here."

"In a coat pocket?" asked the policeman.

"Yes."

"A letter from whom?"

"I—I don't know."

The doctor stepped forward and put a hand on Tod's forehead. Then he looked at the policeman.

"That's enough for now," he said. "He needs to

rest. Tod, it's all right. Don't worry. It will all come back to you. Just rest now."

"Rest," said Tod.

"I'll come back and see you later," said the detective. "Do like the doctor says and get some rest. Okay?"

While Matt Ramsey languished in a tub of hot water and Clarence Dodd lay sprawled on one of the beds in the room, downstairs in the hotel, Lester Wiggins came hurrying in with another man. They spotted Granville Spalding behind the bar and waved him away toward the hotel counter. Spalding turned to the man beside him.

"Take over, Glen," he said, "will you?"

"Sure, Mr. Spalding," said the bartender. Spalding left the bar to join Wiggins and the other man at the hotel counter. They had already turned the hotel register around and were looking at the two latest signatures.

"I guess I know what brings you over here, Em," said Spalding.

"It's him, all right," said the man named Em. "Tod Stover."

"That's what I told you," said Wiggins. "Didn't I tell you?"

"Do you realize what this could mean for the town?" said Em.

"Em," said Spalding, "he couldn't have been more than eight, ten years old then. He might not know anything."

"Yeah, but then again, he might. We got to have a council meeting."

"Well," said Wiggins, "as mayor, you can call a meeting any time you decide."

"I just decided I'm calling one. For right now. Get everyone together."

"Where'll we meet?" asked Wiggins.

"Right here," said the mayor. "Hurry now."

Wiggins rushed out of the hotel, followed by Spalding. The mayor paced the floor nervously for a minute or two, then walked over into the saloon and up to the bar.

"Give me a shot of brandy, Glen," he said.

"Yes sir, Mr. Mayor," said the bartender. He put a shot glass on the bar in front of the mayor and went for the brandy. The mayor drummed his fingers nervously on the bar until Glen returned with the bottle and poured him a shot.

"Just leave it," said the mayor.

"Yes sir," said Glen.

The mayor had downed his second shot when Wiggins and Spalding returned, followed by four other men. He tossed some coins on the bar and joined the six men on the other side of the room.

"The meeting's called to order," he said. "Let's get down to business. Tod Stover's back. You all know what that could mean. Now, Granville's already pointed out to me that young Stover was just a kid when his daddy left town ten years ago and he might not know a damn thing. But then again, he might. And what I'm asking myself is, if he don't know, why the hell did he come back?"

"That's a good question," said Spalding.

"A better question," said the mayor, "is how are we going to handle this thing?"

One of the four newcomers spoke up.

"We could just ask him what he knows," he said.

"No," said the mayor. "We want young Stover on our side. We don't want to jump on him like he's a common criminal or something. We want to make him feel welcome and comfortable here in Lane Rock. We'll give him an official welcome, give him the red-carpet treatment, and we'll just wait awhile and see what he has to say to us. Agreed?"

"Well," said the man who had spoken before, "I don't know. What if he don't say anything?"

"Damn it, Harve," said the mayor, "I didn't say we'd wait forever. I said we'll wait awhile. Are we agreed?"

The six council members muttered their assents, nodded their heads, and looked at one another.

"All right then," said the mayor. "Lloyd and Marvin need to know about this. We can't take a chance on the law harassing these boys."

"I'll tell them," said Spalding.

"Tell them who Stover is," said the mayor, "and tell them how important this is to the town. Tell them to be extra nice to Stover and to his pal, this Ramsey, who come into town with him. Tell them that's an order from the mayor and the town council."

"I'll tell them," said Spalding.

"Now, we don't want to bother those boys this evening," said the mayor. "They just come in off the trail with only one horse between the two of them. But I think that Granville here could send up a couple of steak dinners and a bottle of good whiskey, compliments of the town. How's that sound?"

"That sounds good," said Wiggins.

"I can have that done," said Spalding.

"We're spending town money," said the mayor. "We need a vote to make it legal. Any opposed?"

No one spoke.

"So ordered," said the mayor. "Now, I suggest the town pick up the entire tab here at the Spalding House for those two."

"The whole thing?" asked one of the councilmen. "In addition to the dinners and whiskey tonight?"

"That's what I said," said the mayor. "Any opposed? Good. That's passed. Now, I want every one of you back here in the morning at six. These boys might be early risers. We're going to meet them for breakfast, on us, and give them our official welcome to Lane Rock. Any questions?"

There were no questions, and the meeting was adjourned.

CHAPTER

★ **4** ★

Matt Ramsey and Clarence Dodd appeared at the top of the stairs, and the mayor stood up quickly from his chair.

"Go on, Granville," he said. "You and Lester. Go on. You've both met them. Bring them on over here."

Granville Spalding and Lester Wiggins moved to meet Matt and Clarence as they came down the stairs. The mayor and the other council members stood around a specially prepared table, which had been set up in the hotel-lobby side of the room. It was a long table with nine chairs around it, covered with a clean white tablecloth and prepared with nine place settings. At the foot of the stairway, Spalding spoke first.

"Good morning, gentlemen," he said. "We have some friends over here who would like to meet you.

Both of you. We'd like to buy you breakfast, if you'll allow us."

Matt looked from Spalding to Clarence, his expression conveying cautious curiosity. He looked back at Spalding.

"What's this all about?" he asked.

"A welcoming committee, you might say," said Spalding.

"Official," added Wiggins. "We're the town council—and the mayor."

"I've been in a lot of towns in my life," said Matt, "and nobody ever offered me this kind of welcome before. In fact, a time or two they tried to run me out."

"Oh, well," said Wiggins, chuckling nervously, "I don't blame you for being a bit skeptical. Frankly, Mr., uh, Ramsey, this welcome is really for Mr. Stover here. You're included because you're with him—you're his friend."

Matt looked again at Clarence.

"You didn't tell me you was some kind of big shot in this town," he said. "I guess the railroad folks didn't know that either."

Clarence laughed out loud and slapped Matt on the back.

"Come on," he said. "Let's join them. We can't turn down this kind of hospitality, can we?"

"I don't know," said Matt, but he followed the two councilmen and Clarence over to the table. Wiggins pulled out a chair for Clarence, and Spalding pulled one out for Matt.

"Let me introduce everyone," said Spalding. "Gentlemen, I'd like to present Mr. Tod Stover here,

and his traveling companion, Mr. Matt Ramsey. Mr.
Stover, Mr. Ramsey, this is our mayor, Mr. Emerson
Hubbard. The rest of us here are members of the
town council. You've met Lester Wiggins. This is
Harvel Beck. This here is Eldon Gray. Howard Box.
Clell Harman. Please be seated, gentlemen."

Spalding snapped his fingers in the air and two
waiters appeared, one with a pot of coffee.

"Coffee all around?" he asked. Everyone as-
sented, and the waiter with the pot began filling the
cups.

"This is Danny," said Spalding, indicating the
other waiter. "He'll take your orders. I hope steak
and eggs is agreeable to everyone. Just tell Danny
how you'd like them cooked, and he'll take care of
the rest."

Matt sipped at his coffee. It was good and it was
hot, but he was uncomfortable. He wondered what
this official welcome was all about, and he wondered
when it would come time to pay the bill. Nothing in
this life comes free, he thought. He glanced at Clarence. The young man seemed perfectly content with
all the attention he was getting. More than that, he
seemed a little—smug.

"I suppose you know, Mr. Stover," Mayor Hubbard was saying, "that we're all real glad to have you
back in Lane Rock. We were very fond of your
daddy, you know. He was a public-spirited citizen,
and we've all missed him very much these last ten
years. Is he . . . ?"

"He's dead, Mr. Hubbard," said Clarence. "That's
why I'm here alone."

"I'm sorry to hear that. Please accept my condolences. He was a fine, fine man."

The council members all looked at the mayor, wondering when he would get to the point but afraid to bring it up themselves.

"In fact," said Clarence, "right after Daddy died, I found this letter."

He reached into an inside coat pocket and withdrew the letter he had taken from the unconscious Tod Stover, the Tod Stover he had thought was dead and whose identity he had assumed. He handed the letter across the table to Hubbard. The mayor read it through silently, then cleared his throat loudly.

"Gentlemen," he said, "listen to this. It says, 'To Whom It May Concern in the Town of Lane Rock: The bearer of this letter is my son, Tod, who was only ten years old at the time, but he was with me when I left Lane Rock for good. If you remember me, you know what I did for the town, and you know how important Tod's return can be to all of you. Sincerely, Chad Stover.'"

Hubbard handed the letter to Spalding, who was seated next to him.

"By God, sir," he said, "we do remember, and we do know."

The waiter showed up with the breakfasts and began distributing them while the letter made the rounds, so that each council member could read it over again for himself.

"I recognize old Chad's signature," said Clell Harman, actually wiping away a tear as he passed the letter on. "I must have seen it on a thousand documents."

The letter found its way back to Clarence, who stuck it back in his pocket, and the talk subsided while everyone turned to their steak and eggs. Matt was a little more relaxed: The elder Stover must, indeed, have been a man of some prominence in Lane Rock, so the council and the mayor were welcoming his son back to town. But they also expected something from the son, and Matt wondered what that could be. Oh well, he told himself, it don't concern me. He decided to enjoy the hospitality while it lasted.

Mayor Hubbard waited discreetly until everyone had finished eating and the dirty dishes had been cleared away. All the coffee cups had been refilled, and a few of the men were smoking. Hubbard himself had lit a big cigar. Matt Ramsey rolled a smoke and lit it. Clarence declined the makings but accepted the cigar the mayor offered him. Finally, the mayor spoke.

"Mr. Stover," he said, "I don't mean to rush you into anything, since you've only just arrived in town. But how soon, do you think, might we begin to talk business?"

"Why, uh, Mr. Mayor," said Clarence, "anytime's just fine with me. Right now's as good a time as any."

The mayor perched on his elbows and leaned greedily forward, waiting for Clarence to continue. The eyes of all the councilmen were also on Clarence. Clarence looked around the table from one to another. Matt, too, was curious, although he didn't display the eagerness of the others. Clarence finally realized that everyone was waiting for him to continue the discussion.

"Well," he said, "it looks like I'm on the spot. I'm sorry, gentlemen, if you're waiting for me to unfold some important bit of information. I don't know why I'm here."

"What?" said the mayor.

"What?" echoed six councilmen.

"I mean, I'm here because of Daddy's letter. Obviously he meant for me to come here. But as I told you before, I found the letter after his death. I have no idea to what he was referring. I was hoping that someone in Lane Rock could tell me."

"Oh no," said Wiggins.

"All right," said Hubbard, "just hold on. All is not lost yet. You must know something, or your daddy wouldn't have written that letter. We can tell you what this is all about, and maybe that will jog your memory. I, too, have a letter. My letter, too, was written by your daddy, but mine was written almost ten years ago."

The mayor reached into his inside coat pocket and withdrew a folded piece of paper, which he carefully unfolded on the table before him.

"Ten years ago," he continued, "when you were just a child, your daddy was a member of this council. He was also the town treasurer. The mayor at that time was a man named Kelly Ingram, now deceased. Several of us here before you this morning were on that town council with your daddy, but we were outnumbered by Mayor Ingram's hand-picked appointees. We had a fifteen-member council in those days. Back then there were a number of mines in the area still producing well, and the town was prosperous.

In fact, there was a goodly store of gold in the town treasury."

The mayor paused to let all that soak in while he puffed on his cigar and took a long, loud sip of his coffee.

"Well," he continued, "we had several indications that Mayor Ingram intended to abscond with the gold. I won't go into any details, but we were pretty sure that those were his intentions. There didn't seem to be anything we could do about it, because, as I said, the council was stacked in those days with his cronies. Besides that, the town marshal and his deputies were Ingram's men. And they were bad gunfighters. Those of us here who were on the council back then and your daddy had met in secret and talked this over, but we never came up with any plan. All we did was just voice our suspicions and our fears and agree with each other that it was bound to happen and there wasn't nothing we could do to stop it. Then late one night your daddy disappeared. He took you with him, and, we discovered the next morning, he took the gold, too."

"My daddy stole the gold?" said Clarence, astonished.

"Well, yes and no," said the mayor. "He stole it all right, but a month later I received this letter from St. Louis. I'll read it. 'Dear Em,' it says. 'By now you have probably realized that I got out of town with the gold. I took it because I could think of no other way to keep Ingram and his gang from getting it. I have hid it good, and one day, when Ingram is no longer a threat and Lane Rock once again has an honest government, I will reveal its whereabouts to you or to whomever is there in a position of authority. In case this letter should fall into the wrong hands, I will tell you now that I am just passing through St. Louis, but I will not reveal my final destination. I will somehow keep up with the news from Lane Rock, and when the time is right, you will hear from me again. Your friend, Chad Stover.' Well, Mr. Stover, that's it."

"I see," said Clarence. "So I'm supposed to know something about where Daddy hid the gold?"

"That's what we're all hoping for," said Hubbard, "and that's what that letter you're carrying indicates."

"It does, doesn't it?" said Clarence. "I've been trying to figure out what he meant by that ever since I first found the letter. I—I don't know. I was just ten years old when we left, and I was half asleep. Daddy dragged me out of bed that night we left, and my memory of the events of that night—and the whole trip, for that matter—is really hazy. I can't seem to recall anything about it, except riding at night, all night, and being in a hurry, and being tired and sleepy and wondering what it was all about. I remember I was frightened. I didn't know where we were going. Of course, we wound up in Boston. That's where I grew up. I'm sorry. I just can't remember anything that would be of any use."

"You must," said Howard Box. "He had the gold with him. You were with him. He had to have done something with it, and you must have seen it."

"Take it easy, Howard," said Hubbard. "He's right, though, Mr. Stover. You must know something, or your daddy wouldn't have written that letter the way he did. Maybe if you hang around town a few days, look around, maybe something will remind you. We won't rush you. You relax. Take it easy. But look around while you do. And let us know the minute something comes back to you. Anything. Any little detail of that night or that trip that might help. And any way we can help, you let us know."

"Thank you," said Clarence. "I can't think of anything right now. But I'll do as you suggest. I wouldn't be here if I didn't want to help. You know that."

"Of course," said Hubbard.

"If you're going to do any looking around," said Matt, opening his mouth for the first time since the discussion had started, "you'll need a horse."

"Oh," said Clarence. "I guess that's right."

"I'll take care of that," said Wiggins. "I'll get one ready for you down at the stable just as soon as we adjourn here."

"Thank you, Mr. Wiggins," said Clarence.

"Yes, thank you, Lester," said Hubbard. "Of course, the town will cover the expense. Well, I suppose we're adjourned. Lester, you can go and get that horse ready for Mr. Stover. And, uh, Granville, why don't you take Mr. Stover and Mr., uh . . ."

"Ramsey," said Matt.

"Yes, of course. Mr. Ramsey. Why don't you take Mr. Stover and Mr. Ramsey on a tour of our little town. Show them where everything is. Including my office. And show them where Mr. Stover lived when he was a little boy. Maybe something will help. Even if it doesn't help right away, Mr. Stover needs to be familiar with Lane Rock. It's been a pleasure, gentlemen."

Hubbard shook hands with Matt and Clarence.

"And remember," he said, "anything we can do to help, let us know."

The tour of Lane Rock didn't take long, and when it was done, Granville Spalding excused himself to get back to his business. Matt and Clarence were left alone on the street. Matt gave Clarence a long, hard look.

"Tod, boy," he said, "you've got yourself in a real hot spot here."

"Yeah," said Clarence, "I guess I have."

"Are you playing straight with these people?"

"Yeah," said Clarence, "of course I am. What makes you ask a fool thing like that? You saw the two letters. They were both passed around. You heard the mayor read them. Besides, what could I gain from lying about a thing like that?"

"You're gaining a few days of easy living right now," said Matt. "And I am, too. That's what makes me nervous. That's a part of it."

"Well, I'm straight," said Clarence. "So what else is bothering you?"

"It don't take no time at all for news to travel in a small town like this. I get the feeling already that everyone in town knows who you are and why you're here."

"What's wrong with that?"

"You're supposed to know the secret of where a whole mess of gold is hid. Some people would do most anything to get that kind of information."

"Aw, come on," said Clarence, "these people are real friendly. They want the gold for the town."

"We ain't met them all," said Matt.

"Hey, Matt. If you're scared, you can ride out any time you feel like it. I'll be all right here. Besides, you don't owe me anything."

"I didn't say I was scared," said Matt. "I said I'm nervous, and I am. And I know I don't owe you anything. Just the opposite. But I'm staying anyhow. You got me curious. I want to see this thing played out for some damn reason. Besides, I'm afraid I've taken a liking to you. Come on. Let's go down to the livery and try out your new horse."

CHAPTER
★ 5 ★

Only one road led east out of Lane Rock. It was the same road on which Matt and Clarence had come into the town, the road that ran parallel to the railroad tracks. They rode out anyway, retracing their steps. There was the rise that ran alongside the tracks, and to their south, the road up on the rise. The rest was flat. Not much was there to suggest anything. Just a few miles out of town, Matt stopped.

"This is the way your daddy would have drove out of town that night," he said. "Anything ring a bell?"

"No," said Clarence. "Nothing."

"Well," said Matt, "I didn't think it would. If I was riding out of Lane Rock with a bunch of stolen gold, I don't believe I'd come this way. Not even if I planned to wind up in Boston. There's no place to hide the gold. No place to hide yourself if someone happens to come after you. Come on."

He turned his big black around and headed back for town, Clarence following on the roan gelding that Lester Wiggins had provided. They rode back into town and hesitated there while Matt looked around. The road they came in on continued through the town, where it became the main street; then it went on west and up into the mountains. Nothing left town going south. The prairie was flat and open in that direction. One trail left Lane Rock going north. It appeared to be little used, and it ran through prairie much like that to the south.

"Come on, Tod," said Matt. "Let's try those mountains."

As they rode through Lane Rock, Mayor Emerson Hubbard watched them through a window in his office. It didn't take long to make it all the way through the town, and soon they were climbing. They were not more than twenty minutes out of town when they passed the first of the abandoned mines. It was off to their left, on the south side of the road. The mine entry was boarded over, and off to one side a shack stood, its door hanging by one hinge. Matt stopped.

"One of these old mines would be a likely place to hide something," he said.

Clarence shrugged and raised his eyebrows.

"I just don't know, Matt," he said.

They rode on, noticing right away that they didn't have to climb far into the mountains before there was a considerable drop in temperature. They passed a couple more abandoned mines and one that looked pretty run-down, although it appeared to still be occupied.

"You suppose someone's still working that thing?" asked Clarence.

"Probably so," said Matt. "They said that there was a couple of die-hards up here still scratching at these played out mines."

"The Hard Biscuit," said Clarence, reading the old weathered sign that was tacked above the entrance to the mine.

Matt studied Clarence for some sign of—what? He wasn't sure what it was he was looking for in the young man. He wanted to believe the story Clarence had told: that he had found the letter after his father had died, that he really did not know what the old man had been talking about in the letter, but that he had come out to Lane Rock anyway out of a sense of duty and hoping that some resident would know what the letter was all about. He wanted to believe Clarence when he said that he had only vague memories of the night his father had spirited him out of bed and away from Lane Rock in the middle of the night and for good—or at least for ten years. But something about Clarence bothered him. He couldn't quite define it, but he didn't really trust the likable young man. He kept asking himself what could possibly be wrong. Why was he so suspicious? Clarence had the letter, and it matched the letter the mayor had. The stories fit together perfectly, and it made sense that a ten-year-old boy rudely awakened in the middle of the night would not have a clear memory ten years later of what had happened that night. So what was it that bothered Matt Ramsey? He wasn't sure.

"Anything familiar?" he asked.

"Well," said Clarence, "it does seem kind of like I might have been on this road before. Nothing specific, though."

As Matt and Clarence headed on back down the road toward Lane Rock, two men stepped out of the mine shack there at the Hard Biscuit. The older of the two men, a man perhaps forty-five with graying hair, stood with his hands on his hips, staring hard after the two riders. The younger man spoke.

"That's them, Vernon," he said. "The one in the dude clothes, riding the roan—that's Stover."

"Chad Stover's kid," said the other, "all growed up. Go get your shirt on and get the others together. We're going to town."

Tod Stover finished tying his tie. He felt for the money belt around his waist, then picked up his vest and put it on. The door to his hospital room opened, and the Boston detective walked in.

"Hello, Sergeant Welch," Tod said.

"You remember me," said Welch.

"I remember—most things," said Tod. "Not everything."

"The doc told me you were feeling much better," said Welch. "He said you'd be leaving today. I wanted to talk to you once more before you left."

"I don't know what more I can tell you, Sergeant," said Tod. "I do know who I am, and I remember that I was going to a town called Lane Rock, a place I used to live in when I was a child, because my father wanted me to go. There was something he wanted me to take care of for him, but I don't re-

member what it was. I remember that I was on the
way to the railroad station when I was attacked."

"And you were robbed?" said Welch.

Tod finished buttoning his vest and picked up his
coat.

"I don't remember that," he said, "but I must have
been. I know I had a railroad ticket."

"And a letter," said Welch.

Tod's hand went to his left-hand inside coat
pocket.

"A letter," he said. "Yes."

"Who was the letter from?" asked Welch. "What
was in it?"

"I don't know. That's one of the things I don't
know."

"The man who attacked you," said Welch, "do
you remember anything more about him?"

"No. Not really. Actually, I'm not even really sure
if I was attacked. I was running down the alley. I
was afraid that I'd miss my train, and I just sort of—
ran into this fellow. I think he was as frightened as
I was. And we started to fight. That's all I recall."

"He was probably frightened," said Welch. "You
probably encountered this man right behind the
pawn shop he had just robbed. We found a rock with
blood on it, and we found your hat there, too. The
back door of the pawn shop had been broken into.
The cash register had been robbed and a gun stolen.
You probably surprised him just as he was coming
out."

Tod looked at the hat. Then he put it on his head.
He winced and took it off again.

"Head still sore?" asked Welch.

"Yes," said Tod. "I don't think I'll wear this."

"What did the man look like?"

"It was dark, and he surprised me. But I'd say that he was about my age, about my size. And he was well dressed. I'm afraid that's the best I can do."

Sergeant Welch took a pad and a pencil out of his pocket and began to write. As he wrote, he mumbled.

"Well dressed," he said. "About twenty years old. Five feet eight or nine inches. One hundred and . . . ?"

He paused and looked inquiringly at Tod. Tod shrugged.

"Hundred and sixty-five, seventy," he said.

"Sixty-five or seventy pounds. Probably in possession of an English-made Galand and Sommerville revolver. Might try to sell."

"Is that what he took from the pawn shop?" asked Tod.

"Hmm? Oh, yes. A bit lucky for us, too. It's a rather unusual handgun. Well, Tod, what will you do now?"

"I'm going on to Lane Rock," said Tod. "That's what I was doing when I was interrupted, and besides, it might help me call things back to mind."

"I hope it does," said Welch, offering his hand. "Good luck to you."

Granville Spalding was behind the bar in his establishment when the front door opened and five men with one woman came into the bar. They selected a table and sat down around it. Spalding hurried over to greet them.

"Hello, Vernon," he said. "What brings you all into town?"

"We got a right, ain't we?" said the man called Vernon.

"Well, sure," said Spalding. "Of course you got a right. It's just that we don't often see you—especially all of you. I was just making conversation, I guess. What can I do for you?"

"We didn't come for conversation," said the other. "We come to eat. We want steak dinners. Steak and fried 'taters. And bring a bottle of whiskey. Six glasses."

"Daddy," said the woman, a young woman, in a protesting voice.

"Oh, all right, Rosalie. Spalding, you got a sody water?"

"Yes."

"Bring one of them."

Spalding went back to the bar to get a bottle of whiskey and six glasses. Then he got the soda. As he started back toward the table, he hesitated and spoke in a low voice to his bartender.

"Glen," he said, "go to the kitchen and order up six steaks. Then get over to the marshal's office and tell Lloyd that Vernon Bancroft is here with his whole gang. Hurry."

When the town marshal, Lloyd Stilwell, and his deputy, Marvin Conley, walked into the Spalding House, Bancroft and his party were about halfway through their meal. Bancroft looked up as the two lawmen were walking past his table. He had just jabbed a piece of steak into his mouth.

"So they called the law, did they?" he said. Grease ran down a deep wrinkle that age had drawn from the corner of his mouth to his jawbone.

"Howdy, Vernon," said Stilwell. "Me and Marv just come in for a drink."

"Yeah," said Bancroft, reaching for the whiskey bottle to pour himself another drink. "I'll bet. I bet you come over here to keep an eye on us."

"I don't care what you're doing," said Stilwell, "as long as you behave yourself. All of you. Come on, Marv."

Stilwell and Conley walked on over to the bar, and Bancroft laughed as they walked away. He jiggled his finger at the others around his table.

"Behave yourselfs now," he said. "You heard the marshal."

He lifted the glass of whiskey and downed it in one swallow, then picked up the bottle to refill it. At the bar, Stilwell and Conley ordered their drinks. Stilwell leaned with his elbows on the bar, his back to the rest of the room, but Conley turned around, leaning back on the bar. His eyes were on Bancroft and his group. The front door opened and Matt Ramsey walked in, followed by Clarence Dodd. As they walked past the Bancroft table, Bancroft stopped chewing and stared at them. Matt noticed the stare, but he had sort of gotten used to being stared at in Lane Rock. Everyone was interested in what Tod Stover had in his head about the town's gold. They walked to the bar, and Bancroft leaned over toward the man seated on his left.

"That them, Lon?" he said.

"That's them."

"All right," said Bancroft, his voice low, "everyone take a good look. Them two that just walked in—the one in the dude suit is Tod Stover. Remember him."

"Who's the other one, Vern?" asked a man across the table.

"Never mind," said Bancroft. "He don't matter none. Just remember Tod Stover."

Matt and Clarence had just reached the bar when Stilwell stepped out to meet them. He nodded a greeting.

"Mr. Ramsey," he said. "Mr. Stover. Allow me to buy you a drink."

"Well, thank you, Marshal," said Clarence. "Why don't we find a table?"

"Sure," said Stilwell. He looked at Glen behind the bar and gave a jerk of his head. Glen followed the four men to a table.

"What'll it be, gents?" he asked.

"More of the same for us," said Stilwell.

"I'll have whatever Matt's having," said Clarence.

"Whiskey," said Matt.

Glen left for the whiskey, and Matt settled back in his chair, nervous. He wasn't nervous about anything in particular. He just wasn't used to being treated like a big shot, and he didn't like it. He had decided to see this thing through, however, so he would simply have to put up with this kind of treatment for the time being. But damn, he thought, he would be glad when it was all over and done with. Glen brought the whiskey and poured drinks all around. Then he left the bottle on the table and went back to the bar. Matt held up his glass as if for a toast.

"Thanks," he said.

"It's all right," said Stilwell. "You two went out for a ride today."

"Yeah," said Clarence.

"I reckon everyone in town knows every move we make," said Matt.

Stilwell laughed a quick, nervous laugh.

"Well," he said, "yeah. You're right about that. We *are* keeping pretty close tabs on you, but it's just because we're all interested in Mr. Stover's memory. You understand."

"Yeah," said Clarence.

"Well, before you ask," said Matt, "we didn't do no good out there today. And it might make everything a little more comfortable in the meantime if you'd stop calling us 'mister.' I'm Matt, and this here is Tod."

"Well, all right," said the marshal. "I'm Lloyd, and this is Marv."

"That's a heap better already," said Matt. "I believe I'll have me another drink, and then we can think about ordering us some lunch. What do you say, Tod?"

"That sounds good to me," said Clarence. "Will you gentlemen join us?"

CHAPTER

★ 6 ★

Bancroft grabbed one of his men by the arm and led him outside to the street. He pushed him up against the wall in front of the Spalding House and looked up and down to see if anyone was near. Satisfied, he shoved his face up close to the other's ear.

"Leo," he said, "do you think that old Spalding there would give my Rosalie a job waiting on tables or something?"

"Why, I don't know, Vernon. I guess he might, if you was to ask him."

"We got to get Rosalie away from the mine," said Bancroft. "I don't trust her with what we've got to do."

"What're we going to do, Vernon?"

"Never you mind just yet. Just listen to me and do what I say. We need someone in town, too, to listen around for us, let us know what's going on.

But we got to be careful how we ask Rosalie, so she don't get suspicious. Now, I'm going back in there and ask Spalding if he'll put Rosalie to work. Then we'll get her a room here. You can bring her things on back in to her after a while. Let's go back now."

They went back inside, and Bancroft walked over to the bar. He sidled up to Spalding and shoved his hand in his trouser pocket.

"I want to pay up, Spalding," he said.

"All right."

"And I want to ask you something."

He pulled his hand out of his pocket and dropped a handful of change into Spalding's hand. Spalding counted it, and separated some of the coins. He reached to hand some back to Bancroft.

"That's too much," he said. "This here's yours."

"You keep it," said Bancroft. "A—what you call it? A tip, for good service. For putting up with me and the boys."

He laughed at his own joke, and then he looked down at the floor.

"What is it you wanted to ask?" said Spalding.

"Well, you see, it's like this. My Rosalie, she's getting too old to be staying with a bunch of men out at the mine. I got to watch her all the time. Oh, not because of *her*. She's a good girl. It's because of *them*. I can't trust them around her. She needs to move into town and get a town job. Something respectable. I was wondering if you could use some help around here. She'd work hard. If she didn't, I'd whip her good."

"Well, Vernon," said Spalding, "I—I don't know. I hadn't thought about hiring on anymore help. I . . ."

Spalding looked back at the table at which Rosalie and Bancroft's cronies were still sitting around. Rosalie was a nice-looking young woman, and it was a shame to think of her living out there at the mine with those . . . Well, living out there at the mine. In addition, he wondered what Bancroft and his boys might do if he refused his request. Of course, the marshal and the deputy were in the saloon, but there was always later. He glanced toward Stilwell and Conley, and he noticed Matt and Clarence sitting there with them. He thought about the special treatment he was having to give to those two. A waitress might not be a bad idea.

"Tell you what, Vernon," he said. "We'll give it a try—say for two weeks. See how it goes. Rosalie can have a room right here in the Spalding House. We'll call it part of her pay. She can eat here, too. Bring her on over to the counter there, and I'll get her a room."

"Thank you, Mr. Spalding," said Bancroft, grinning and pumping Spalding's hand. "Thank you, sir."

"You see that feller there with Mr. Spalding?" said Conley, his voice low and confidential.

"Yeah," said Matt. "He's with that bunch over there by the door."

"That's right," said the deputy. "Just a word to the wise: When you're out and around, watch out for them. They're a rough bunch. Vernon Bancroft is the old man. The girl, Rosalie, is his daughter. The rest are a bunch of hardcases he picked up somewhere: Melvin Hartley, Leo Wilcox, Lon Truitt, Irvin Carter. They stay out at the old Hard Biscuit Mine. Supposedly they're scratching a living out of it, but I think that damn mine played out years ago."

"We'll keep it in mind," said Matt. "Right now I want something to eat."

By the time Matt, Clarence, Stilwell, and Conley had eaten their meal, Bancroft and his men had left town and Rosalie was settled in her new room just across the hall from the one in which Matt and Clarence were housed. Spalding had told Rosalie to relax a bit. When she felt like it, he had said, she could come down and he would begin to show her around and acquaint her with her new job.

It was late that night when Leo Wilcox returned from the Hard Biscuit Mine in a wagon with a trunk loaded with Rosalie's belongings. He pulled up in front of the Spalding House and locked the brake on the wagon. Then he climbed down off the seat, moved around to the back of the wagon, and dragged out the trunk, hefting it up on his back. He struggled up to the front door of the Spalding House and shouldered it open, then banged his way on in. Spalding was behind the counter on the hotel-lobby side of the big room. He looked up from his work.

"This here is Miss Rosalie's stuff," said Wilcox, puffing. "Vern sent me in with it."

"Oh," said Spalding. "Her room is just at the top of the stairs. First room on your right. Number six."

Wilcox staggered up the stairs and dropped the trunk on the floor there before number six. Then he banged on the door, and Rosalie opened it.

"I brung your stuff, Miss Rosalie," said Wilcox.

"Oh, thanks, Leo," said Rosalie. "Come on in."

Wilcox dragged the trunk into the room. He straightened up and smiled at Rosalie.

"I'm just glad to do it," he said. "Vernon told me to, but I'd have been glad to do it anyhow—for you."

"Thank you. It's fine right where it is. I need to unpack now. I'm okay. You can go on back."

"Aw," said Wilcox, "I ain't in no hurry. I can help you unpack that stuff and get it put away."

"No thanks, Leo," said Rosalie. "I don't need no help."

"Well," said Wilcox, a grin spreading over his face, "maybe we could just visit a spell."

He turned quickly and shut the door behind him.

"Leo," said Rosalie, "what are you doing?"

She moved toward the door to open it again, but Wilcox blocked her way.

"This here's the first time we ever had a chance to be alone together," he said. "Your old pappy was always there in the way, a-watching you like a hawk. He ain't here now."

"Leo," said Rosalie, "I appreciate you bringing my things in, but you better go now."

"I don't want to go," he said, and he reached for her, but she dodged away from his grasp.

"Leo," she said, "go!"

He reached for her again. She tried to get away, but he managed to grab her left arm. She struggled, but he pulled her roughly to him and reached around her with both arms.

"Come on, Rosalie," he said. "Be nice."

"Let me go!"

He pressed his face against hers, and his slobbering

lips found her mouth and sucked at it greedily. She tore her face away and spat at him. Wilcox suddenly released her and gave her a hard slap across the face. She cried out in surprise and pain, and while she stood there stunned, Wilcox lunged at her, his weight bearing both their bodies down onto the bed. His hands found her breasts and squeezed and mashed, and his slobbering mouth again pressed against her unwilling lips.

Downstairs in the bar, Matt Ramsey tossed down one last shot of whiskey.

"I'm turning in," he said.

Clarence Dodd was surrounded by a number of citizens of Lane Rock, who had been buying his drinks. He enjoyed being treated like someone really important, and he wasn't ready to call it quits.

"I'll be up later, Matt," he said.

Matt thought that Clarence had had enough to drink, but he decided that it wasn't his place to tell another grown man what to do. Let him find out for himself. The young fool would have a hell of a hangover in the morning. It might teach him a lesson. Matt went to the bar and reached into his pocket.

"It's on the house," said Glen.

"I've had about enough of this 'on the house,'" said Matt. "How much do I owe you?"

"Mr. Spalding says that I ain't to take none of your money."

Matt pulled out a handful of change and looked at it. Then he tossed it on the bar.

"Call it a tip," he said. Then he turned and walked

through the bar to the hotel side of the room. Spalding was still there at the counter.

"Good night, Mr. Ramsey," he said.

Matt lifted a hand in response. Then a scream ripped through the hotel from upstairs. Matt shot a questioning glance toward Spalding.

"Rosalie Bancroft," said Spalding. "I put her just across the hall from you."

Matt raced up the stairs, taking three steps at a time. At the top of the stairway, he turned quickly to his right and opened the door. Wilcox was on top of Rosalie on the bed. Rosalie was struggling to get out from under him. Wilcox was so intent on his wickedness that he didn't even hear Matt come in. Matt took two long steps across the room to stand just at Wilcox's feet.

"Hey, mister," he said.

Wilcox half turned and sat up on the edge of the bed, his eyes opened wide. Before he had time to get over his surprise, Matt swung a hard right that connected with Wilcox's jaw and knocked him over sideways. He fell off the bed and landed on the floor with a crash. Trying to get up, Wilcox managed to raise himself to his hands and knees, and Matt grabbed his shirt collar and his belt and lifted him off the floor. Wilcox screamed and flailed his arms and kicked his legs, but Matt walked out into the hall with him and, at the top of the stairs, gave a heave. Wilcox sailed about halfway down the stairs screaming. Then he landed on his belly and skidded down a few more stairs before he managed to squirm over onto his back. His feet went up over his head, and then he rolled head over heels the rest of the way down, landing at the foot of the stairs on his back, his feet resting on the bottom step. He looked up and saw Matt Ramsey standing on the landing above. Matt turned to go back to Rosalie and make sure that she was all right. Wilcox pulled his old Remington .44 out of its holster and cocked the hammer.

"Ramsey!" shouted Spalding. By this time Clarence had heard the commotion and had run out of the bar. He saw Matt spin around and drop to one knee, pulling out his Colt and cocking it all in one motion. Wilcox pulled the trigger and sent a shot crashing into the doorframe just above and behind Matt. Matt squeezed the trigger. The bullet smashed into Wilcox's sternum, but because of the angle of the shot, it exited at the base of his neck in back and buried itself in the floorboards. Wilcox gave a jerk, then relaxed and lay still. A pool of blood began to spread itself on the floor from beneath his body. Matt stood up and stared down at Wilcox. He knew that he had killed the man. He holstered the Colt and walked to the doorway of number six.

"Miss Rosalie, is it?" he said. "Are you all right, ma'am?"

"I'm—yes," said Rosalie. "I'm all right. Thank you. Did you . . . is Leo . . . ?"

"He's dead," said Matt. "Keep your door shut and locked. If you need anything, I'm just across the hall."

He stepped back out into the hallway and pulled the door shut behind him, then listened as she fastened the inside latch. He stepped back over to the landing at the top of the stairs and looked down.

"If anyone needs me," he said, "I'll be in my room."

Standing beside the body at the bottom of the stairway, Spalding and Clarence watched Matt until he disappeared into the room. Then they looked at each other.

"I never saw anything like that before in my life," said Clarence. "Never."

"I wouldn't expect you to, living in Boston," said Spalding, "but I never have either. He's fast. Fast and straight."

The front door opened, and Lloyd Stilwell came in, followed by Marvin Conley.

"What's happened here?" asked the marshal.

"Matt just killed this fellow here," said Clarence. "You should have seen it."

"Where is he?"

"He's gone to his room," said Spalding. "Said if anyone needed him, he'd be there."

Stilwell looked at the body, then looked at Spalding.

"Do I need him?" he asked.

"I don't think so, Lloyd," said Spalding. "Ramsey was just on his way upstairs to turn in for the night. He just passed by me here at the desk when we heard a scream from upstairs. It was Rosalie Bancroft. This here, uh, Leo Wilcox it is, had gone up a few minutes earlier with her trunk. Old Vernon had said that he'd be sending her stuff in by someone, so I didn't think anything of it. But when we heard her scream, Ramsey tore right on up there. Pretty soon he had tossed Wilcox headlong down the stairs. I never saw anything like it. Tossed him halfway down the stairs in the air. Then he just turned his back on him. Wilcox was on the floor, right where he is now, and he pulled out his shooter. I yelled at Ramsey, and Ramsey dodged Wilcox's shot. His was truer. That's just how it happened."

"I saw it too, Marshal," said Clarence. "It happened just like Mr. Spalding here said."

"Well," said Stilwell, "I should get a statement from Ramsey and one from Miss Bancroft, but I guess it can wait until tomorrow. No need to bother them any further tonight. Marv, get some help and get this out of here. We'll ride out to the Hard Biscuit in the morning and tell old Bancroft what happened here tonight. I guess he'd want to know."

"God," said Clarence, "I never saw anything like that in my whole life."

CHAPTER
★ **7** ★

It was early morning when Stilwell and his deputy mounted up and prepared to ride out to the Hard Biscuit Mine, but they hadn't any more than turned their horses to head west into the mountains when they saw Matt Ramsey and Clarence Dodd, also mounted.

"You're out early," said Stilwell.

"We figured you'd be riding up to see Bancroft," said Matt.

"That's right," said Stilwell. "So?"

"We're riding along with you."

"Now what the hell you want to do that for?" said the marshal.

"I killed the man," said Matt. "If there's going to be any trouble over it, I ought to be there."

Stilwell looked from Matt to Clarence.

"And you?" he said.

"I'm with him."

"All right. Hell. Come on," said Stilwell, and he started riding toward the mountains without looking back to see who was following and who was not. A half-hour ride found them at the entrance to the Hard Biscuit Mine.

Bancroft heard them coming, and as they rode up to the shack, he stepped out the door, a shotgun in his hands. Melvin Hartley stood on his right with a carbine. To his left, a six-gun in each hand hanging down at his sides, stood Lon Truitt. Irvin Carter was in the doorway.

"What the hell's this all about?" asked Bancroft.

"Your man Wilcox," said Stilwell.

"He ain't here. He didn't come in last night."

"He's dead," said Stilwell.

"How?"

"I killed him," said Matt.

Bancroft turned his shotgun toward Matt.

"He was trying to rape your daughter," said Stilwell. "Ramsey here stopped him."

"Well," said Bancroft, "if I'd a caught him at that, I'd a killed him myself. Is that all?"

"That's it," said Stilwell. "Just thought you'd like to know."

"All right then," said Bancroft, "you told me. Now you can go on back to town."

"You want the body?" asked Stilwell.

"What the hell would I want with it? The son of a bitch tried to molest my little girl. Throw him out in the field and let him rot. Let the gophers eat him,"

Melvin Hartley giggled. "And the coyotes," he added.

"Buzzards," said Lon Truitt.

"Maggots," said Irvin Carter.

"Come on," said Stilwell. He turned his horse around to ride back out to the road, and the others, except Matt, followed. Matt slowly backed his big stallion away from Bancroft and his gang. Only when he had reached the road did he turn it to ride along and catch up with his companions. As soon as Matt was beyond hearing, Bancroft spoke.

"That's one less hand to help do the job," he said. "And one less way to split the loot."

Tod Stover had arrived at the railroad station early the second time and he purchased a ticket all the way to Lane Rock. Somewhere out on the central plains, he sat and mused as the train rushed him westward. He tried to recall his mission, but he couldn't. He thought about his father, a fine man, and he remembered well his father's recent death and funeral. He also remembered that his father, on his deathbed, had called him to his bedside and given him a letter to take with him to Lane Rock. There was something that his father had wanted to do, but, lying on his deathbed, he knew that he would never get it done. He wanted Tod to do it for him. It was important. It had to be done. It had something to do with the time ten years before when they had left Lane Rock. All that he remembered. It had come back to him while he lay in the hospital in Boston, recuperating from the blow to his head. But just what it was that his father had wanted him to do he could not call back to mind. He kept telling himself that being back in Lane Rock would help bring it back to mind.

He remembered sitting beside his father's bed and holding his father's hand. "Don't worry, Dad," he could remember saying. "I'll get it done for you." But what was "it"? He couldn't remember. He couldn't. Damn. He recalled the scene as clearly as if it had occurred just yesterday, and he distinctly remembered that he had been perfectly confident in his ability to do just what he had promised.

But what was it that he had promised? That he did not know. Blast that nameless wretch who had attacked him in the alley. Robbing a pawn shop. Indeed! No, he thought. Blast me! If I had gone to the station early, the way I should have done, none of this would have happened. That poor rotter was as surprised as I was. He just got the better of me in the fight, that's all. He tried to relax, to put it all out of his mind, but he couldn't. He kept straining to remember. Finally he lay back against the seat and turned his head to look out the window and watch the West rush past him.

The sun was low in the west when Vernon Bancroft and his gang rode into Lane Rock and tied their horses in front of the Spalding House. Bancroft led the way inside. He pointed to a table on the bar side of the room.

"Sit there," he said.

Glen came to the table. "Can I help you?" he asked.

"Why ain't my Rosalie waiting on tables?" said Bancroft.

"She worked a full day already," said Glen. "She's off now. What can I get for you?"

"Give them a cup of coffee each," said Bancroft. "No booze."

"Aw, Vern," said Truitt.

"You heard me, God damn it," said Bancroft. "Drink coffee! I don't want no one drunk tonight. You hear?"

"I hear you," said Truitt.

"I'll tell on anyone who has a drink," said Hartley.

"Good," said Bancroft. Then he turned back to Glen. "Where's my little girl? I need to talk to her."

"She's probably upstairs in her room, Mr. Bancroft. Number six, I think it is. At the top of the stairs."

Bancroft gave one more warning look at his cronies and walked across the room to the stairs. He stomped on up and looked at the first two doors he saw.

"Number six," he said out loud, and he knocked. Rosalie opened the door.

"Daddy!" she said.

Bancroft pushed his way into the room and sat down on the edge of the bed.

"I heard you had a little trouble with Leo last night," he said. "I'm sorry about that. If I'd a knowed he'd try a damn fool thing like that I wouldn't have sent him in here to you. But it's all right now, I guess, 'cause he's dead."

"It's all right, Daddy," said Rosalie. "He didn't hurt me. Mr. Ramsey threw him out before he got a chance to—well, to do what he wanted to do."

"Mr. Ramsey?"

"Matt Ramsey," said Rosalie. "He lives right across the hall. With Mr. Stover."

"Mr. Stover," said Bancroft. "There used to be a Mr. Stover lived here a long time ago. I kind of remember him. Would it be the same feller?"

"No," said Rosalie. "This one's a young man. But you might be remembering his daddy. His daddy used to be the treasurer for Lane Rock. Everybody's talking about it."

"About what, baby?"

"Mr. Stover, the old one—he stole the town's gold, but he only done it to save it, 'cause the mayor was going to steal it. Not Mr. Hubbard, but the mayor that they had back then. Now that the old crooked mayor's dead, Mr. Stover wanted to give back the gold, but only he died first, so his son, young Mr. Stover, Tod, he came to town. But he can't remember where the gold is hid."

"He can't?"

"No, he can't."

"Well," said Bancroft, "if you're okay, I reckon I'll run on along back to the mine. You know, I can't trust them boys that I got working for me. Have to watch them all the time. I'll see you later, baby."

"All right, Daddy," said Rosalie. "Good night."

Bancroft went back downstairs and joined his gang at the table. He leaned forward on the table and motioned to the rest to do the same. When they were all leaning inward conspiratorially, he spoke to them in a harsh whisper.

"Stover has told them he don't remember where the gold is hid," he said.

"He don't?" said Truitt.

"He says he don't," said Bancroft. "I don't believe that. Not for a minute I don't. He's up to something."

Over near the bar at another table, Matt Ramsey and Clarence Dodd sat with Lloyd Stilwell and Mayor Hubbard. Spalding joined them now and then, but he kept jumping up to check on things behind the bar. Matt had just downed a whiskey. He stood up.

"I'm turning in," he said.

"It's early, Matt," protested Clarence.

"Well," said Matt, "it seems to me like it's kind of late. In more ways than one. I'm pulling out in the morning. First thing."

"Pulling out?" said Clarence. "You said you'd see this thing through with me."

"I know I said that, but I didn't figure it'd take you so long to remember that hiding place. You don't need me. I'm just a drain on the town's treasury, and I don't like that feeling. I'm used to paying my way."

"Matt," pleaded Clarence, "give me another day or two."

"Tod, we've rode all over this town and all over the countryside around it. I don't know what we can do that we ain't already done. I'm leaving in the morning. Good night, gentlemen."

He turned and left the bar. Clarence poured himself another drink, while Hubbard stared at him.

"He's making sense, you know," said Hubbard.

"What?" said Clarence.

"How long is it going to take for you to recall the events of that night? Will you ever remember? This is not a rich town, Mr. Stover, and we can't continue to support you in this fashion indefinitely."

Clarence tossed down his drink. He was beginning to feel lightheaded.

"Of course you can't," he said. "I—I never expected you to. Just give me a little more time. All right? Things are getting to seem more familiar to me every day. Another couple of days, I bet it'll all come back to me."

"All right," said Hubbard, throwing a sideways glance at Stilwell, "we'll wait a bit longer. I believe Ramsey had the right idea, though. I'm heading for the house."

"I need to check on Marv," said Stilwell. "See you later, Tod."

Clarence found himself suddenly alone. He didn't like the feeling. He enjoyed all the attention he had been getting as Tod Stover, and he liked the companionship of Matt Ramsey. He had to think. He'd had it real good here in Lane Rock, and he didn't want it to come to an end. What if he could find that gold? But the people of Lane Rock were bound to have searched everywhere for it over the last ten years. How could he find it when they hadn't? He had to think of something, though. Otherwise Matt would ride out in the morning, and in another day or so, Hubbard would decide to cut off the water. He had to think of a way to extend his stay in Lane Rock. Or at least to leave with money in his pockets. That would be tough. The town had been spending money on him ever since they found out who he was—or, rather, who he was impersonating. Sitting there alone with a bottle of whiskey on the table before him and his head starting to spin, Clarence began to feel desperate. If he couldn't come up with a plan, he would have to just sneak out of town before they caught onto him. He needed a clear head. He couldn't think straight in this condition. Tomorrow. Tomorrow he would plan it all out. He felt the call of nature, and he stood up unsteadily.

"Glen," he said, "I'll be back. Leave my bottle here. Don't let anyone get it, either. Okay?"

"I'll watch it, Mr. Stover," said Glen.

Clarence staggered over to the long hallway at the end of the bar that led out back. Outside, he stopped and took several deep breaths of fresh night air, then headed for the outhouse. Two figures lurked in the shadows behind the hotel. They eased their pistols out of their holsters and looked at each other there in the dark alley. A couple of minutes passed.

"He's been in there a long time," said Melvin Hartley. "Reckon we ought to check on him?"

"Just shut up and wait," said Lon Truitt. "I ain't following no one into a backhouse. You seen how drunk he was. Maybe he's puking."

Just then Clarence stepped out. He stood for a moment, trying to get his balance and clear his head. Then he started walking toward the hotel, toward the back door he had come out through. His path was not straight, and his steps were not steady. Once he almost lost his balance, and he stopped for a moment in another attempt to regain his composure. Then he lurched forward again. He was almost to the door, and he was already reaching out with his right hand for the door handle, when the two men stepped out of the shadows, one on each side of him.

He saw the guns, and he felt a hand grab hold of each of his arms.

"What—" he began.

"One more sound out of you, mister," said Truitt, "and you're dead. You understand me?"

Clarence nodded his head stupidly.

"You just come on along with us, and you won't get hurt. Come on."

Truitt and Hartley turned Clarence away from the hotel and started walking in the shadows. Clarence was drunk. He was afraid that he would be sick. And he was frightened.

CHAPTER

★ 8 ★

Truitt and Hartley were back inside the Spalding
House within an hour. They strolled in, trying very
hard to seem casual, and they resumed their seats at
the table with Bancroft and Irvin Carter. Bancroft
passed them the whiskey bottle he and Carter had
been sharing, and he spoke in a low voice.

"You get him?" he asked.

"Yeah," said Truitt.

"Any trouble?"

"Nope."

"Anyone see you?"

"Nope."

"You put him where I told you?"

"Yeah."

"Good. We'll stick around here an hour or so.
Maybe get good and drunk. Make sure everyone

knows we're here. That'll give us an alibi—just in case."

"What about," began Harley, "well, you know. What about—him?"

"Leave him be for now," said Bancroft. "Let him sleep off his drink. Let him wonder what the hell's going on. Let him have a good hangover and get good and hungry. Get scared. It'll soften him up for us."

It was about midnight when Spalding came back into the bar after taking care of some hotel business. The Bancroft gang was still at the table, still drinking. Spalding gave them a sideways glance as he spoke to Glen at the bar.

"Everything all right here, Glen?"

"Yeah," said Glen. "No problems. Bancroft and them has been real good tonight. Just setting there a-drinking. Keeping to themselves. Only one thing."

"What's that?" asked Spalding.

Glen pointed at the bottle and the glass on the table where Clarence had been sitting earlier.

"Tod Stover left out of here a while ago to go out back," he said. "Told me to watch his bottle. Said he'd be right back. I ain't seen him since. Course, he was pretty drunk."

Bancroft stood up and stretched, then he walked over to the bar and tossed some coins down.

"That cover it?" he said.

"Yes sir, Mr. Bancroft," said Glen. "Thank you."

"Best get my boys home," said Bancroft. "Got work to do in the morning."

Bancroft led his gang out the front door, and Spalding moved to a front window to watch as they mounted up and rode out of town. Then he went back to the bar.

"I'll check out back," he said.

Glen busied himself with cleaning up the bar for closing. Bancroft and his cronies had been the last customers. In a few minutes, Spalding came back.

"I thought maybe he'd passed out back there or something," he said, "but there ain't no sign of him."

"You suppose he could have got upstairs without me knowing it?" asked Glen.

"Maybe," said Spalding. "I don't think so, though, and I hate to wake up Ramsey to find out. Aw hell, he could be anywhere. Let's let it go until morning. If he ain't showed up by then, we'll report it to Lloyd."

Clarence Dodd did not know where he was. He had been taken somewhere outside of town. He knew that much. His head was still spinning from all the whiskey. Damn, he thought. I should have gone to the room with Matt. But "should have" didn't count for anything, and he was somewhere up in the mountains in a shack that smelled musty and old. It was dark, so he couldn't be sure, but he didn't think that the shack had been lived in for some time. The very air seemed dusty. His hands had been tied behind him, and he had been thrown down on an old bed—a cot, really—that was covered with dust. Then his feet had been tied together. He thought about struggling to free himself, but the room was spinning around him. He decided that he had better simply try to sleep off his hangover and hope that he woke up sober before his captors returned. He was too drunk to be terribly frightened, and soon he drifted off into drunken oblivion.

Matt Ramsey was up early the next morning. He noticed that the man he knew as Tod Stover was not in his bed and had not slept in it the night before. But he recalled that the young man had been having a whooping good time in the bar. He might have found himself a better place to spend the night, with a cozier roommate. Or he might be passed out on the floor downstairs or out back or even out front in the street. He was pretty well on his way to sense-lessness, as Matt remembered. He shrugged it off and packed his saddle roll. It would be a long trail to somewhere else, and he wanted to get an early start.

Downstairs, Spalding was behind the hotel counter.

"Check me out, Mr. Spalding," said Matt, walking past. "I'm getting myself some breakfast, and then I'm hitting the trail."

"Ramsey," said Spalding, "wait a minute."

Matt stopped and turned to face Spalding.

"Is Tod Stover upstairs?"

"He didn't come in last night," said Matt.

"Then I'm afraid he's disappeared."

"Disappeared? Hell, he's a young man with a wild streak. He was having a good time last night. He could be anywhere."

"Glen said he went out back last night, just a little while after you left. Told Glen to watch his bottle and said he'd be right back. No one's seen him since."

Matt tossed his saddle roll down on the counter.

"Damn," he said. "That boy had better be in trouble."

"What?"

"If he's pulling a stunt on me to keep me from hauling out, I just might kill him. Have you talked to the marshal?"

"Not yet," said Spalding. "I was waiting to see you."

"Well, let's go see him then."

Matt headed for the door without waiting to see whether or not Spalding was following. Spalding hurried along behind him. In a few minutes they were at the marshal's office, where Marvin Conley was busy making coffee.

"Lloyd ought to be here any minute now," said the deputy. "He usually shows up about this time. You want to wait?"

"No," said Matt. "We're going on back to the Spalding House. I don't want to wait for your coffee. Tell him we'll be waiting for him down there."

"What's this all about?"

"Tod Stover has disappeared," said Matt, and he walked out of the office. Spalding looked at Conley, looked after Matt, shrugged, and hurried out the door.

"Disappeared?" repeated Conley, but there was no one left in the office to answer him.

Matt had just finished his breakfast and was drinking another cup of coffee when Stilwell came in. Spalding saw him and followed him over to the table where Matt was waiting.

"What's this about Stover?" asked Stilwell.

"He didn't come in last night," said Matt.

"He left the bar early, Glen said," added Spalding. "He just went out back, you know, and he told Glen he'd be right back. We ain't seen nothing of him since."

"All right," said Stilwell. "Let's not go off half-cocked. Might be nothing's wrong. I'll get Marvin, and Ramsey here can help. We'll look around some. See if we can come up with him somewhere."

"I'll go along for a while, Marshal," said Matt, "but don't forget one thing."

"What's that?" asked Stilwell.

"That boy's supposed to have the secret to the whereabouts of a whole lot of gold locked up some-wheres in his head. Some men would do a lot to unlock a secret like that."

"Damn it, Ramsey," said Stilwell, "I know that. I'm thinking the same thing you are. But let's be sure he's not just laid up drunk or with some little gal before we get all excited. All right?"

"All right," said Matt. "For now."

"By the way," said Stilwell, looking at Spalding, "Bancroft and his bunch were in town last night, weren't they?"

"Yeah," said Spalding, "but they couldn't have had anything to do with this. Stover disappeared early. Bancroft and his boys were here until we closed last night. Around midnight."

Clarence woke up with a throbbing headache. He felt a little sick, and he felt a voracious hunger, but mostly his head hurt. He turned one way and another in an attempt to relieve the pain, but nothing seemed to help. He groaned out loud, and he felt like crying. Then the door opened and Vernon Bancroft walked in, followed by Hartley, Truitt, and Carter.

"How you feeling, friend?" said Bancroft.

Clarence groaned. "I think I'm sick," he said.

"Sick, hell," said Truitt. "The little shit's hungover."

Melvin Hartley giggled.

"A man who can't take it shouldn't drink whiskey," said Carter.

"If he can't take it, he ain't a man," said Truitt.

"Shut up, boys," said Bancroft. "Our friend here ain't feeling good. I bet a little food would make him feel better. How about it there, Mr. Stover? You want some breakfast? That make you feel better, you think?"

"I am hungry," said Clarence.

"Lon," said Bancroft, "build up a fire and heat up them beans we brought over. And make some coffee. See that he gets fed good. We got a lot to talk about, and Mr. Stover here needs to be in good shape. Mr. Stover, I'm real sorry we had to bring you out here the way we done, but really, we're your friends. We all want the same thing. You eat and get to feeling better. We'll talk a little later. Ain't no hurry. Lon, you do like I said, you hear? Melvin, you stay here with Lon. Me and Irv will be back later on. Take good care of Mr. Stover there, you hear?"

Bancroft and Carter left the shack, and Truitt began building a fire in the old stove.

"Well, don't just stand there," he said to Hartley. "Go get the damn beans and the coffee. And don't forget the coffee pot. Do I got to do it all? Hell!"

"Shit," said Hartley. He kicked at the floor and stomped his way back outside. Truitt shot a mean glance at Clarence.

"You're a hell of a lot of trouble," he said. "All I got to say is that you better be worth it. You better lead us to that gold. If you don't, I'm going to cut open your belly. Personal. You hear me, boy?"

Clarence groaned.

"And you can just shut that up," said Truitt. "I don't want to hear it. Just shut up."

Hartley came back in with the beans, coffee, coffee pot, and a pan.

"Well, put some water in the damn pot," said Truitt. Hartley took the pot and went back outside while Truitt attacked the can of beans with his skinning knife. In spite of themselves, Truitt and Hartley soon had hot beans and hot coffee. It was about as sorry a breakfast as Clarence could remember having in a long time—maybe ever—but he ate it with relish. He was hungry. And it did help his head. The throbbing was not as bad as before. He finished a second plate of beans and a fourth cup of coffee, and he wiped his mouth on his sleeve. He was sitting on the edge of the cot, his feet still tied together, but his hands had been freed so he could eat.

"Thanks," he said. "I feel much better."

"Well," said Truitt, "I don't give a damn about that myself, but Vern said he wanted you feeling better, so it's a good thing. You want more coffee?"

"Yes, please," said Clarence.

Truitt stepped over to the cot and poured Clarence another cup.

"That's about it," he said. "Melvin, go get some more water in this pot."

Hartley took the coffee pot and went back outside. Clarence took a sip of the coffee Truitt had just poured him. He reached down and set the cup on the floor.

"I've got to go outside," he said.

"Go outside?" said Truitt.

"Yeah. Four cups of coffee. And I've been tied up here all night before that."

Clarence began rocking back and forth on the edge of the cot.

"Oh, all right," said Truitt. He stepped over to Clarence and untied the ropes that bound his legs together. "Go on," he said. "Right around back. Hurry up."

Clarence walked out the door. He was a little unsteady on his legs, partly because of his overindulgence of the night before and partly because his legs had been tied for several hours. Just as he stepped out the door, he met Hartley coming back in. Hartley dropped the coffee pot, spilling water out onto the ground, and he pulled out his revolver. With his left hand he grabbed Clarence by the shirt front.

"Where the hell you think you're going?" he said.

Truitt came out the door.

"He's going to piss, damn it," he said. "Watch him. I'll fix the damn coffee."

"Oh," said Hartley. "Well, go on."

Clarence walked around to the back of the house. Hartley stopped just around the corner and leaned on the side wall.

"Hey, boy," he called out. "That's what got you in trouble last night."

He giggled at his joke.

"You ought to learn how to control that better," he said, and he laughed again. "Sound like a race-horse."

He paused, but then he realized that he heard nothing.

"Hey, boy," he said.

He got no answer.

"Stover!"

He stepped around to the back of the shack. Clarence was nowhere in sight.

"Stover!" he shouted. "Where the hell are you?"

Truitt heard the shouts and came running around to the back of the shack.

"Damn!" he said. "You let him get away? You dumb bastard!"

"He was right here just a minute ago," whined Hartley.

"Come on," said Truitt. "Only one way he could have gone."

Both men pulled out their revolvers, and they ran down a narrow footpath that led off into the rocks behind the shack.

"There he is," said Hartley, and he fired a shot. Up ahead on the path, Clarence hollered, staggered, and fell forward.

"Damn you!" said Truitt. "You better hope you didn't kill him. If you did, Vern'll kill us both."

CHAPTER

★ 9 ★

They met back in Lloyd Stilwell's office: Stilwell, Conley, Matt Ramsey, and Spalding. Stilwell sat behind his desk while Conley took a chair against the wall and Spalding paced the floor. Matt leaned against the doorframe and rolled a cigarette. For a moment no one spoke.

"I can tell by the way you're all looking that nobody had any luck," said Stilwell.

"He ain't nowhere in town," said Conley. "If he was in town, we'd have found him. We been to every house and every place of business. Even every empty building. He ain't here."

"That means someone got him," said Spalding. "Someone who wants to get the gold for himself."

"I hope you're right," said Matt, "but there is one other possibility."

"What's that?" asked Stilwell.

Matt took a long draw on his cigarette and let the smoke out slowly.

"Right from the beginning I had a bad feeling about that boy," he said. "Something don't seem right. Mayor Hubbard applied a little pressure yesterday. Maybe Tod don't know where the gold is. Maybe he never did. Maybe he skipped out on you."

"No," said Spalding. "I don't believe that."

"You don't want to believe that," said Matt.

"Ramsey," said Stilwell, "that's a funny way to talk about your friend."

"Don't get me wrong," said Matt. "I like the boy, but I don't know him any better than you do."

"You rode into town with him," said Conley, his voice accusing.

"I just met him out on the trail," said Matt. "He had just got himself throwed off the train. I picked him up."

"The little bastard," said Conley. "Living off us that way. Pulling a scam."

"All I said," said Matt, "is that there's another possibility. We don't know that's what happened. He still might have got himself kidnaped. The horse he's been riding is still in the livery stable. Any other horse missing?"

"Not so far as we know," said Stilwell.

"There ain't been a train or nothing else leave town since Tod was seen in the bar, has there?"

"No."

"I don't think he'd leave town on foot," said Matt. "Probably our first notion is the right one. But we need to keep open minds. That's all."

Spalding was still pacing the floor. He stopped and looked directly at Stilwell.

"Then what's our next move?" he asked.

"Well," said the marshal, "we've looked everywhere in town. We'll have to expand our search. Start looking out. I'll get some more men. We'll send some out in every direction. Marv, you take Ramsey there and head up into the mountains. Check those old abandoned mines. Anyplace else you think about or come across. That all right with you, Ramsey? You still with us?"

"I'm with you," said Matt.

"Let's go then," said Conley.

Matt turned and walked out the door, followed by the deputy. They mounted their horses and headed west.

The shrill whistle of the train cut into the normal quiet of Lane Rock's atmosphere, and people from all over town ran toward the station to watch the train pull in, some just for the variety and entertainment, some curious to see if the rails had brought any new customers for the local economy. Several passengers got off and headed for the business district of the town. None were carrying luggage. The general assumption was that all were therefore transient. They might buy themselves a meal before the train pulled out again, but that would be about it: a boost only to the economy of a few eating establishments. Still, the arrival of the train and the presence of strangers in town created some excitement. Most of the disembarked passengers went to the Spalding House, and of those who went in, all but one went immediately to tables to order something to eat. Rosalie Bancroft began hustling from one table to another, taking the orders. As busy as she was, she noticed the young man who did not come to a table. Instead, he went to the hotel counter on the other side of the room. He was a handsome young fellow, she thought. He was wearing a suit that gave him the appearance of an eastern dude, but he wore no hat. There was a bandage on one side of his head.

She finished taking the orders at a table full of customers and she turned the orders in to Glen. She had other customers still waiting, but she was worried about the young man. Spalding was out with the search party, looking for the missing Tod Stover, and Glen was too busy to notice anyone at the hotel counter. Spalding had not bothered finding a replacement clerk for the hotel, as he hadn't expected much business over there. So Rosalie made her other customers wait a little longer and she trotted over to the counter.

"Hi," she said.

"Hello," said the young man.

"There's nobody working the hotel right now," she said. "Did you want a room?"

"Yes, I do."

"Well, why don't you sit down in there and have something to eat or something," suggested Rosalie. "Mr. Spalding will be back soon."

The young man looked hesitant.

"There's nothing to worry about," said Rosalie. "There's plenty of rooms. You'll get one. If Mr. Spalding don't get back when this rush is over and the train leaves, Glen can fix you up. He's the bartender. He's just too busy right now. And I am, too. I got to get back."

"Thank you," said the young man. He watched her hurry back to her job. A pretty little thing, he thought. He followed her and found himself a table.

The crowd of transient passengers ate quickly when they got their food, and soon it was as if they had never been there, except for the one remaining, who sat alone at a table and drank coffee. Rosalie walked by his table with dishes she had cleared away from other places.

"Thanks for waiting," she said. "I'll tell Glen."

She carried the dishes into a back room, then stopped at the bar.

"Glen," she said, "that gentleman wants a room, and Mr. Spalding ain't come back yet."

"I'll take care of him," said Glen. "Just take a minute."

He walked over to the young man's table.

"Rosalie says you want a room, mister," he said. "If you'll come with me, I'll get you fixed up."

They walked over to the hotel desk, and Glen turned the book around for the new guest to sign. Then he turned his back to get a key.

"I'll put you in number eight," he said. "It's just up at the top of the stairs and a couple of doors down. Something wrong?"

"It appears," said the young man, "that someone has already registered for me."

"What?"

"My name is Tod Stover."

• • •

Clarence Dodd writhed in pain back on the filthy cot, and Lon Truitt worked futilely to stop the bleeding from the hole Hartley's .44 slug had torn in his right shoulder. The door opened and Hartley came in, pushed from behind. Bancroft stepped in next.

"Damn fools!" he said. "I can't leave you for a minute. How the hell's he going to do us any good in that shape?"

He grabbed Truitt by the shoulders and flung him aside.

"Get out of my way," he said. "I'll take care of that. I've patched up enough bullet holes in my day, I guess."

Bancroft started working on the wound. Truitt, feeling wrongly abused, sulked against the wall.

"I didn't shoot him," he said.

"You was supposed to keep your eye on him. On him and on Melvin. Melvin ain't bright, you know."

"He was running away," said Hartley. "What was I supposed to do?"

"In the first place," said Bancroft, "you was supposed to watch him so he wouldn't get a chance to run away. Then when you made your first mistake, and he was running, you should have run after him and caught him. Now both of you get the hell out of here and let me work in peace! Hang around outside, though. I might need something."

Clarence groaned.

"It ain't too bad, son," said Bancroft. "I'll get you fixed up here in no time. You just trust me. I know what I'm doing. I've fixed them up worse than this. You'll be just fine, boy, just fine."

Bancroft probed the wound, and Clarence cried out in pain.

"Take it easy," said Bancroft. "You shouldn't have tried to run. I'm sorry my boy out there shot you, but you shouldn't have done that. Hell, I wasn't going to hurt you. Just ask you some questions. Now look at the mess we've got."

The searchers returned to Lane Rock just about the time Mayor Hubbard and the members of the town council—all except Spalding, who was coming in with the search party—were arriving at the Spalding House. Glen had run to the mayor with the startling news that the Spalding House now had a second guest with the name of Tod Stover. Hubbard saw the riders coming back into town, and he waved frantically at them.

"Come on in here," he shouted. "We're having an emergency town council meeting right in here in the Spalding House. I want you here too, Lloyd, and you, Ramsey. Right now."

Hubbard stomped inside the hotel.

"Glen," he said, "invite your new guest to our meeting here. Then you can go on back and tend your bar."

He selected a table in the back of the bar for privacy, and the others followed him. Soon the entire town council, the marshal, and Matt Ramsey were seated. The second Tod Stover walked in. He looked over the group inquisitively.

"Mayor Hubbard?" he asked.

"That's me," said Hubbard.

"I understand you'd like to see me? I'm Tod Stover."

There was near pandemonium around the table. Hubbard called for order several times and banged on the table with his fist before the astonished makeshift committee could quiet down again.

"Yes," said Hubbard. "Mr.—Stover, I'd like very much for you to join us at this here meeting."

The mayor offered Stover a chair next to his own, then introduced everyone around the table by name.

"Now, Mr. Stover," he continued, "the reason these gentlemen here were so astonished to hear your name is that they, some of them, have just returned from being on a search party looking for a missing person, a person who has been here in our community for just a short while and who introduced himself to us by the name of Tod Stover. He also told us that he and his father were former residents of Lane Rock and that his father was our former town treasurer, Chad Stover."

"Chad Stover was my father, gentlemen," said Tod. "I'm sorry to say that he recently passed away."

"The other Mr. Stover," said the mayor, "had in his possession a letter written by Chad Stover. We compared the signature on that letter to one on a letter in our files that we know to be authentic. The letter was indeed written by Chad Stover. How do you explain that, sir?"

"I think I can explain that very easily," said Tod. "I was surprised when I started to sign the hotel register here and saw that the last name entered was my own, but now it's all coming together."

"I wish you would make it so clear to the rest of us," said Hubbard.

"Just before my father died," said Tod, "he gave me a letter, and he told me something that he wanted me to do. It had something to do with Lane Rock. We had lived here ten years ago, and he had been a member of the town council. I believe that he was also the treasurer. I think you mentioned that a moment ago, Mr. Mayor."

Hubbard nodded and grunted an assent.

"When my father died, I sold all our household goods, packed my bags, and bought a ticket west on the railroad, intending to come out here and fulfill his last request. I had most of my money in a money belt around my waist, but I had a few dollars in change in my pockets. I had my ticket, which was only for part of the way here, in my coat pocket, and I had my father's letter here, in my inside breast pocket. I had stopped to get myself a meal before leaving Boston, and I noticed that it was later than I had thought. I was about to miss my train. I ran down an alley in order to get to the station quicker, and there I ran into another man. He was just coming out the back door of a pawn shop. We startled each other, I think, and we began to fight. Then he knocked me unconscious with a rock."

"Uh, hold on just a minute there," said Hubbard. "This fellow that you fought with—what'd he look like?"

"He was about my age, I'd say," said Tod, "and about my size. He was well dressed. I would guess that he was a fellow Bostonian, well to do, who had fallen on hard times. Anyway, when I awoke there in the alley, I had no idea who I was or where I was. The blow to my head had caused temporary amnesia. I was eventually picked up on the streets by the police and taken to a hospital. In a few days my memory began returning to me, and I think I'm almost completely recovered."

"How do we know," asked Lester Wiggins, "which one is telling the truth? We have two men, both claiming to be Tod Stover."

"I have my identification here," said Tod, reaching for his wallet. "My attacker must have been frightened away. He didn't finish robbing me. He took my train ticket, my pocket change, and the letter from my breast pocket. Fortunately, he didn't get either my wallet or my money belt."

He handed the wallet to the mayor.

"All right," said Hubbard. "You've got the wallet and he's got the letter. We still have a dilemma."

"Tell us what it was your father wanted you to do here in Lane Rock," said Matt.

"That's the one thing I haven't been able to remember since the blow to my head," said Tod.

"Damn!" said Hubbard. "Neither one of them remembers. What the hell do we do now?"

"You could contact the Boston police to verify my story," said Tod. "They told me the man had just robbed the pawn shop when I ran up on him. He got a little money out of the cash register and he stole a gun. Then he got a little more money off of me and my ticket and the letter. They never found him. I expect that he caught the train, using my ticket. I imagine that he's the one who signed my name to the register."

"Do you know what kind of gun he stole?" asked Matt.

"Who cares?" said Spalding.

"I do remember," said Tod. "I heard the detective mention it. He said that it was a bit unusual and might help them catch the fellow. It was an English-made Galand and Sommerville revolver. I forget the caliber."

"It's a .450," said Matt. "Gentlemen, this man is Tod Stover."

"How do you know that?" asked Wiggins.

"First off, he said he bought a ticket only part way. I picked up the other fellow out on the prairie just after he'd been tossed off the train. Second, I seen that Galand and Sommerville rig that he stole. This is Tod Stover, all right. The other man's an impostor."

CHAPTER
★ 10 ★

The meeting broke up and the bar at the Spalding House was almost deserted. Glen remained behind the bar, and Rosalie was still there to wait on any customers who might come in. Spalding himself went back to the hotel desk. Tod Stover stood alone uncertainly for a moment. Then he turned to Rosalie.

"Are—are you still serving food?" he asked.

"Sure," said Rosalie. "You want to eat?"

"I thought that I'd wait until the rush was over. Everybody else seems to be gone now. Is it all right?"

"Yeah. If I don't have any customers it looks like I don't have anything to do. Mr. Spalding might decide that he don't need me around. What would you like?"

"Do you have a menu?"

"A what? Oh, a menu. No. But we have steak and

potatoes and eggs. We have biscuits and bacon and sausage and brown gravy."

Tod suddenly became bold.

"Have you had your dinner yet?" he asked.

"Me?" said Rosalie. "Not yet, but that's all right. I can take care of you first. There's plenty of time before we'll get busy again."

"Why don't you turn in two orders of whatever you think is the best thing you have, and then you could sit down and eat with me."

Rosalie blushed slightly. She ducked her head and looked down at the floor.

"I don't know," she said. "I probably shouldn't."

"You just told me there's plenty of time before you get busy again. Please. I really hate to eat alone."

She looked at him. He looked a little funny, she thought, with that bandage on the side of his head, but other than that, he was a handsome fellow. Young. And he was dressed so well. He must be rich, she thought. And he's such a—a gentleman.

"I'll ask Glen if it's okay," she said. "If he says it's okay, then I'll do it."

Rosalie turned to go back to the bar, and Tod raised his voice just a little to call after her as she walked away.

"If he doesn't say it's okay," he said, "I'll have a word or two with him."

He watched her as she walked up to the bar. She was really a lovely young thing. A bit rough, but he liked that in her. Ten years in Boston had taken the rough edges off of young Tod Stover, but they hadn't taken his memories of the West away from him. They hadn't taken away his love of the wild country and the rugged people of the West. He had been taken away from Lane Rock at the age of ten. He had not had a voice in the move, and he had not liked it. His father had told him that it was necessary, and he had believed his father, but it had taken him several years to begin to accept his life in Boston. He had insisted well into his midteens that he hated Boston and the entire East. But he was young, and he had adapted. Now a young man and on his own, his choices his own to make, he had returned to Lane Rock. He had a task to perform, and he didn't know what he would do with himself once that was done. He thought that he wanted to remain in Lane Rock, but he had no job, and the money he had with him wouldn't last forever. Well, he would worry about that when the time came. In the meantime, he would do his job and enjoy being back home, and this young woman seemed such a natural part of Lane Rock.

She was talking to the bartender now, and both of them shot a glance in his direction. Tod smiled and nodded. Then Glen disappeared into a back room, and Rosalie came hurrying back to Tod with a coffee pot.

"I guess you'll want another cup of coffee while you wait for your dinner," she said.

"Yes," said Tod. "*My* dinner, or *ours*?"

"Ours," said Rosalie. "When it's ready I'll bring it out, and then I'll sit down with you and eat."

"Thank you," said Tod. "That's wonderful."

She poured the coffee and then went back to the bar, only to vanish into the back room where Glen had gone. Tod thought she had a marvelous way of moving. Yes, he told himself, I will have to settle down here.

Vernon Bancroft pulled a chair up close to the cot on which Clarence lay in pain and perspiration. Bancroft leaned over Clarence so close that Clarence could feel the older man's hot, fetid breath against his cheek. He turned his face to the wall so that he would not have to look at the wretched old man.

"Stover," said Bancroft, "how's the shoulder?"

"It hurts," said Clarence.

"You think you can tell me where the gold is?"

"I can't remember," said Clarence.

"I ain't going to doctor you and feed you forever, boy. You better start remembering."

"Mr. Bancroft," said Clarence, "take me back to town. Let me go. You don't want me. My name is Clarence Dodd. I'm not Tod Stover. I don't know anything about the gold."

"You're not Tod Stover?" said Bancroft. He looked over his shoulder at Truitt, standing back a few paces. "He says he ain't Stover, Lon. What do you think about that?"

"He thinks we're stupid," said Truitt. "Just tell us he ain't Stover and we'll turn him a-loose."

Bancroft grabbed Clarence's face in his rough old hand and pinched it and turned it toward his own.

"Listen to me," he said. "If you ain't really Stover, then there ain't no reason for me to keep you alive. If you fooled us, and you really ain't who I think you are, I'll just leave out of here and never bother you again. I'll leave Lon there to finish you off."

"I'll carve you," said Truitt. "No need to waste no bullets."

"Now, I'll ask you one more time," said Bancroft. "Whatever you tell me now, I'll believe. What's your name?"

Clarence looked at Bancroft's leering face, and he looked past Bancroft at Lon Truitt, leering viciously at him and fingering his long skinning knife.

"Tod Stover," he said. "I'm Tod Stover."

"All right," said Bancroft. "Now we got that straight, where's the gold?"

"I really can't remember," said Clarence. "I—I think I can find it, though, if I ride around up here. It's in an old mine shaft. Yes. I remember now. It's in an old mine shaft."

"Which one?"

"I don't know. It was dark. I was only ten years old, and it happened ten years ago."

"Go ahead and cut him, Lon," said Bancroft, starting to get up from his chair. Clarence grabbed the old man's arm.

"No!" he said. "Wait. I'll know if I see it. All we have to do is ride around. Ride by the old mines. I'll recognize it when I see it. I know I will. "

He released his grip on Bancroft's arm and fell back on the cot with a groan. Bancroft studied Clarence for a moment.

"Get him his dinner, Lon," he said. "We'll let you rest the day out and the night. In the morning we're going for that ride. And we better come up with something."

Bancroft stood up and went to the door.

"And don't start to feeling frisky," he said. "I ain't

leaving you with just these slow-witted boys of mine no more. I'm only just going outside. I ain't going far."

Bancroft left the shack, and Truitt busied himself with preparing the meal as he had been instructed to do. Clarence lay on his back and stared at the ceiling. He felt feverish, and he was afraid. What would he do in the morning? He could waste a certain amount of time just riding the roads and looking, but Bancroft would tire of that quickly, he knew. How long could he run this bluff? At last the thought that had been in the back of his mind formed itself into words. This may be my last night on earth, he thought. It had seemed like a good idea, a good scam, and he had lived high on the hog for a few days, he and his new buddy, Matt Ramsey. But now it looked as if he would die soon. A few days of luxury and being treated like royalty had not been worth the final cost. He was burning up with fever, and his shoulder hurt with a throbbing pain. He thought of his father, the father he had treated so badly. He wished that he could see old Horace Dodd one more time, just long enough to—to tell him that he was sorry for the way he had been. If Bancroft were to kill him in these mountains, Horace would never even know what had become of his errant son. Tears came to Clarence's eyes, and he wiped them quickly. He didn't want Truitt to see them.

Spalding went into the bar to get himself a cup of coffee. He got a cup, but Rosalie had already gotten the pot and was refilling the cups at the table at which she had been eating with Tod. Spalding carried his cup back to the table.

"You have enough in there for me too?" he asked.

"Sure, Mr. Spalding," said Rosalie. She filled his cup.

"Would you join us?" offered Tod.

"Well," said Spalding, "for a couple of minutes, I guess. Thank you."

He pulled out a chair and sat down across the table from Tod. Rosalie had returned the coffee pot, and she again took her place at the table.

"Mr. Spalding," said Tod, "do you know where the house in which I used to live with my father is?"

"Sure," said Spalding.

"Is it occupied?"

"Nobody has lived in it since you left. Just go out here on the main street and head west. It's the last house on the south side of the street. Right on the edge of town. It looks pretty run-down, as you might guess. Ten years. You can still tell, though, that it used to have green paint on it."

"I'd like to go down there and take a look at it," said Tod. "Do you think it would be all right?"

"Oh," said Spalding, "I'm sure it would."

Tod took another sip of his coffee, and he looked at Rosalie over the edge of the cup. He lowered the cup.

"Will you walk down there with me?" he asked her.

"I can't, Tod," she said. "I'm working. Well, I know it don't look like it just now, but really I am."

"It's all right, Rosalie," said Spalding. "We're not busy. Take a little time off if you like."

"Well," said Rosalie, "all right. Just let me clear all this away, and I'll be ready to go."

She cleared away the dishes and took them to the back room.

"She's a lovely girl," said Tod.

"Yes," said Spalding. "I can't imagine how or why, knowing her father."

"What's he like?"

"He's an old reprobate. A miner, supposedly, but I wouldn't put anything past him. Not even murder."

"She's coming back," said Tod, in a low voice. He stood up as Rosalie approached the table.

"Are you ready to go?" he asked.

"Yeah."

"Mr. Spalding," said Tod, "thank you, and I'll see you later."

Tod felt good strolling down the street with Rosalie. He was in his favorite place, a place full of fond memories, and Rosalie was a beautiful young woman. People's heads turned as they saw Tod and Rosalie. Tod knew why. They knew who he was and why he was in town. They were naturally interested in his goings and comings. But they also knew Rosalie, and undoubtedly, like Spalding, they knew who and what her father was. Tod supposed that there would be quite a bit of gossip around Lane Rock that evening concerning Tod Stover and Rosalie Bancroft. He smiled. Let them gossip.

"There it is," said Rosalie. "You used to live there?"

"I was only ten years old," said Tod.

They stood for a moment and stared at the house from the road. Spalding was right. Evidence of the old green paint was still discernible—barely. Tod tried to tell himself that he recognized the house, but he really knew better than that. Had he not been told where to find it, he would probably have just walked right past it. The front door was off its hinges, and the roof over the porch had fallen in at one corner.

"Let's look inside," said Tod.

They walked up onto the porch and on into the house carefully, fearful that they might step through the floor or that something might fall down on their heads. Dust was thick everywhere in the house, and spider webs were strung here and there. There was some furniture in the house, but it was not fully furnished. Tod figured that people must have helped themselves after he and his father had left in such a hurry, and that what was still in the house no one had wanted or it had been too much trouble to cart away.

"Does it seem familiar to you?" asked Rosalie.

"Yes," said Tod. "Somewhat."

He walked across the room and opened a door into another room. Looking through the doorway, he saw an iron bedframe.

"My room," he said.

"What?" said Rosalie.

"This was my room. That was my bed. It's still here. After all these years."

His mind traveled back ten years to the night that was on everyone's mind in Lane Rock, the last night he had ever spent in that bed. He remembered his father shaking him awake, pulling him out of bed and hurrying him to get dressed. Then they packed

some of their clothes. His father said that they could
only take a few things. They had to hurry. He didn't
know what time it was, but it was dark outside, and
his father had a horse and buggy out there waiting.
And besides the bags with their clothes in them, there
was something else in the buggy. It was—the gold.
Then they drove out of town. They drove . . .

"I've seen enough," he said. "Let's go."

CHAPTER
⋆ 11 ⋆

Matt Ramsey walked into the marshal's office. Stilwell was behind his desk, alone in the office.

"Hello, Ramsey," he said. "Cup of coffee?"

"Thanks, Marshal," said Matt. He pulled a chair out from against the wall and sat down while Stilwell poured the coffee. The marshal handed him a cup, and Matt took a long sip.

"When's the next search party going out?" he asked.

"Who we searching for?" asked Stilwell.

"What do you mean, who, Stilwell? You know damn well who."

"Give him a name then," said Stilwell.

Matt stood up. He walked to the marshal's desk and put his cup down.

"You mean that you're just going to drop the search?" he asked.

"Ramsey," said Stilwell, "we looked for that fellow when we thought he was Tod Stover. He ain't Tod Stover. So we ain't looking."

"You only try to help out when there's a profit in it for the town? Is that it?" said Matt. "What kind of law officer are you?"

"Now hold on," said Stilwell. "In the first place, we don't have any evidence of any kidnaping having taken place. We got a man missing—that's true. But he's a man that attacked the real Tod Stover back in Boston and robbed him. He showed up here and pretended to be Tod Stover. Now, someone like that, I figure he just slipped off and ran out of here before we could catch up with him. And if we did go out looking for him, it would be to throw him in jail. So I figure we're doing him a favor by just forgetting the whole thing."

"I don't see it that way, Stilwell," said Matt. "I think some folks who think that he is Tod Stover snatched him to try to make him tell them where the gold is hid. I think his life is in danger. Maybe he does need to be in jail, but he don't need to be murdered."

"Well, you bring me evidence of a crime, and I'll look into it. Meanwhile, if you're so worried about him, you go look around all you want."

"Thanks for the coffee, Marshal," said Matt. He turned and stalked out the door. Stopping on the board sidewalk, he rolled himself a smoke and lit it. He drew in a lungful of smoke, held it a couple of seconds, and then let it slowly seep out. Stilwell was right. He knew that. So why was he so angry at the marshal? Why did he care so much? The phony Tod

Stover had lied to Matt just the same as he had lied to everyone in Lane Rock. Matt didn't even know the young man's name. So why didn't he just put the whole thing out of his mind and ride on? He tried, but he couldn't answer that question. The young man was likable. That was all. That was . . . No. It wasn't all. The thing here in Lane Rock wasn't finished. It wasn't done yet, and Matt Ramsey wanted to see the end of it.

He walked down to the livery stable and saddled his black stallion. He would go along with the marshal for a time. Perhaps the impostor had run out. Perhaps he had sensed that the game was about to be up. Matt would work for the time being on that assumption. The only logical way out of town would be to the east. He would ride out that way and look for any sign of the fugitive or any sign that he had gone in that direction.

Tod Stover was back at the old Stover house. It was looking more and more like home. He had an urge to start cleaning up, both around the outside and on the inside. He wanted to put a fresh coat of green paint on the house. It was home. And somehow it seemed appropriate that it was in such a state, for that was the way that Tod felt. He felt footloose, rootless, homeless. He felt like he needed to put— well, he thought, to put his house in order. He went inside. His father's big chair used to sit in that corner. He stared at the spot, now bare, and tried to picture the big chair sitting there, his father relaxing in it. He couldn't quite conjure up the picture, and that frustrated him. Father hasn't been gone all that long, he thought, and already I'm forgetting what he looked like. He walked back into his own old room, and once again, he tried to recall the details of that night ten years before. He remembered the rude awakening, the hurried dressing, the getting into the buggy in the light of the stars. He remembered racing through the night. And that was it. He tried to recall more detail, but he couldn't. His head began to hurt. He put both hands to his head and pressed hard. He moaned out loud with the pain, and finally he left the house.

He walked back through town to the Spalding House. Spalding was behind the counter. Tod walked over to him.

"Mr. Spalding," he said, "who owns my old house?"

"Why, uh, I'm not real sure, Mr. Stover," said Spalding. "As far as I know, it's still in Chad's name—your father's. I'd guess that you own it. We can check over at City Hall."

"I'd appreciate it," said Tod.

"Well, come on. Let's go right now."

There was nothing east of town, no evidence of any kind that anyone had passed that way for a while. Matt had not really believed that he would find anything anyway. He continued to believe that the young man he had befriended had been captured by someone and was being held. Whoever had the fellow thought that he knew the location of the gold. They did not know that he was an impostor and that he would have no way of knowing. The man's life was in grave danger. Matt knew that. And even though the man was a liar and a thief, Matt couldn't help but like him. He would have to keep looking. He stopped in front of the Spalding House and tied the black to the hitching rail. He thought that he would go inside and talk to Glen. The bartender seemed to have been the last person to see the fake Stover before he vanished. He knew that the marshal had already talked to Glen, but maybe there was something he had overlooked. It was worth a try.

Matt was about to open the door to go inside when Marvin Conley approached him.

"Ramsey," said Conley.

Matt stopped and turned to face the deputy.

"Yeah?"

"I want to talk to you."

"You're talking."

"Now that we know that your buddy is a fake, I don't have to be nice to you anymore."

"Is that right?" said Matt.

"I never liked you from the first," said the deputy. "I think you and that partner of yours were in this whole thing together. I don't know just what you had planned, but you were going to rob this town blind somehow or other. As it turned out, all you got was a few days' free rent and some free meals and booze. I ought to run you in."

"On what charge?"

"Conspiracy and attempted robbery. Fraud, maybe," said Conley.

"It's a good thing for you," said Matt, "that your boss has got some brains. You sure ain't got any."

Conley slowly pulled out his revolver and aimed it at Matt.

"Maybe I'll just kill you then," he said. "Right now."

"How will you explain a bullet in the back to your boss?" said Matt, turning his back to the deputy and reaching for the door to the Spalding House. He pulled the door open and walked in. Out on the sidewalk, Conley stood with his gun in his hand, alone and with no one to shoot at. He yelled at the top of his voice.

"Ramsey!"

Matt walked into the bar. Rosalie was wiping tables, and Glen was behind the bar. There were no customers. Matt touched the brim of his hat as he passed by Rosalie and walked up to the bar.

"Hello, Mr. Ramsey," said Glen.

"Howdy, Glen."

"Can I get you a drink?"

"No, thanks. I just came in to talk to you."

"All right," said Glen. "What about?"

"The night that Tod—uh, the fake Tod Stover—disappeared."

"I told the marshal everything I know. He was in here kind of late. Got pretty drunk. He went out back to relieve himself. Said he'd be right back, but he never came. That's all."

"Who was in here?" asked Matt. "Who else besides him?"

Glen leaned across the bar toward Matt and lowered his voice.

"By then it was just Rosalie's old man, Vernon Bancroft, and his gang. That's all."

"And they were sitting here the whole time?"

"Till way after that fellow had left," said Glen.

"Wait a minute. Two of them left for a while and came back later. The old man was here the whole time. The old man and Carter. The other two, Hartley and Truitt, they went out for a spell and then came back. They were all four here until I closed the place up."

"Were Hartley and Truitt in here when that fellow went out back?" said Matt.

"I don't believe so, now that I think about it," said Glen. "No. Whenever he went out back, it was just Bancroft and Carter sitting there."

"Thanks, Glen," said Matt. "That's what I needed to know."

"You think they snatched him?"

"It looks damned suspicious," said Matt. "Don't it?"

As Matt stepped back out onto the street, he found himself facing Conley. The deputy, red in the face from anger, was standing in the middle of the street, facing the door.

"Pull your gun, Ramsey," he shouted.

"I've still got business in this town," said Matt. "I don't want to kill no lawman. Not yet, anyhow."

"Draw, Ramsey."

"I won't. You going to kill me anyway? That'd be murder, Marv. Can you handle that?"

"You don't call me by my first name, Ramsey," said the deputy. "You ain't no friend of mine."

"I'll call you 'Marv' or some other four-letter word," said Matt. "Take your pick."

"Damn you. Go for your gun."

"Forget it," said Matt. He walked down to the

hitching rail and reached for the reins of his black. Conley opened and closed his fists two or three times. He knew that Ramsey was right. He couldn't just shoot the man down in cold blood and get away with it. Not even his deputy's badge would allow him that kind of freedom. Angry and frustrated almost beyond his endurance, he ducked his head and ran at Matt. Matt was caught by surprise. He didn't think of the deputy attacking him with bare hands, didn't believe that the man had that much courage. He had bluffed him out of the gunfight, twice, and he thought that was the end of it, at least for the time being. So Conley caught him off guard. The sudden impact of the deputy's bodyweight and the force of his rush carried both men over the hitching rail and onto the sidewalk on the other side. Matt landed on top and rolled away, springing to his feet. He pulled out his Colt and aimed it at the lawman's midsection.

"All right, Marv," he said. "If this is what you want, it's all right with me, but unbuckle that gunbelt."

Just then Stilwell approached the two men.

"What's going on here?" he said.

"Your boy here is itching for a fight," said Matt. "I just thought that it would be better if no guns were involved."

"Is that right, Marvin?" asked the marshal.

"Just let me at him, Lloyd," said the deputy. "I'll break his damn ribs."

Stilwell sighed heavily and walked over to his deputy.

"Let me have your gun," he said.

The deputy unbuckled his gunbelt and handed it

to Stilwell, who then turned toward Matt. Matt already had his Colt holstered and the belt unbuckled. He handed the rig to Stilwell.

"Just remember, Marshal," he said, "I didn't ask for this."

"You been asking for it since you first came to town," said Conley. He doubled up his fists and moved toward Matt. Stilwell stepped back out of the way.

"Come on then, Marv," said Matt.

Matt sidestepped the deputy's first wild swing and waited for the next one. Embarrassed, the deputy caught his balance and began to dance around Matt like a prizefighter. He jabbed with his left, and Matt stepped back out of range. Conley jabbed again, and Matt caught the wrist. Giving it a sharp twist, he wrenched the arm around into a hammerlock behind the deputy's back.

"Ah!" Conley shouted in pain, surprise, and anger. "Turn me loose and fight!"

Matt raised his leg and planted a boot on the deputy's backside, then turned loose the arm and gave a hard shove with his foot. The deputy sprawled out on his face in the dirt. He scrambled to his feet and rushed Matt again. This time Matt was ready. He stepped aside and shoved with both hands on Conley's back, adding to the deputy's velocity and smashing him into the front wall of the Spalding House. He looked over at Stilwell.

"He just won't quit," he said.

Stilwell shrugged.

Conley turned around, blood running from his nose.

"Damn you!" he said. He took another wild swing, which Matt dodged easily, but Matt was getting tired of this game. He drove a right into Conley's gut and the man doubled over, gasping for breath. Matt took a handful of the deputy's hair and pulled him up straight again. Then he drove another fist deep into the breadbasket. He drew back his right, thinking to smash it into the side of the deputy's face, but he hesitated. Conley was still doubled over, still gasping. Matt looked again at Stilwell, and he turned loose the deputy and let him fall to his knees.

"That's enough," said Matt.

"I'd think so," said Stilwell.

Matt once again turned his back on the deputy and walked over to the marshal. Stilwell handed Matt his gunbelt, and Matt buckled it around his waist. He turned and walked back to where the black stallion stood, calmly waiting. He loosened the reins from the hitching rail and put a foot into a stirrup. Both his hands were on the saddlehorn. Conley, meanwhile, had managed to recover his breath. He stood up and staggered toward Stilwell.

"That was a damn fool thing for you to do," said Stilwell, as Conley took his gunbelt in his left hand. The deputy then pulled the revolver out of its holster and leveled the barrel at Matt's back. He thumbed back the hammer.

"Ramsey!" shouted Stilwell.

Matt threw himself backward into the dirt, and Conley's bullet went high, kicking up dust a few feet behind where Matt had fallen. The stallion snorted and danced back into the street. His Colt was out and Matt was rolling. Conley's second shot would

have hit its mark had he not moved. Damn him, he
thought. Why is he making me do this? He cocked
the Colt and pulled the trigger. The bullet crushed
Conley's sternum and slammed him up against the
front wall of the Spalding House. The deputy stood
there for an instant, an expression of disbelief on his
face, his right arm still extended in front of him but
the fingers going limp, the gun barrel pointing at the
ground just in front of him. The fingers relaxed more,
and the revolver slipped from them and fell to the
boards of the sidewalk. The expression went blank,
and the head fell back loosely. Then the body
dropped to its knees, then slowly pitched forward.
And that was all.

CHAPTER
★ 12 ★

Tod bought brooms and cleaning rags and soap, and he and Rosalie carried water to the house. They swept and they dusted. They washed walls and window sills and doorframes, and they mopped the floor. They were both dirty and sweaty, but the house began to look better.

"I think it will clean up and be just fine," said Rosalie.

"It needs some fixing, too," said Tod. "Some carpentry work here and there. I'll need to get the well checked and the, uh, the little house out back."

"Clean up the yard," she said.

"Paint the house. I want to use the same green. I want it as much as possible just the way it used to be."

"Well," said Rosalie, "the house is still sound. It'll fix up as good as new."

"It's awfully nice of you to help me," said Tod. "I don't know what I can do to repay you."

"You don't need to repay me," she said. "I'm just glad to help. You're a nice man. I like you. I guess— I want you to stay around, and this is my way of helping to make sure that you do. That's all."

She embarrassed herself with what she said, and her cheeks flushed a little. Tod saw the red, and he smiled. He wanted to step up to her, put his arms around her, and press his lips to hers. He wanted to, but he didn't. It wouldn't have been proper, and besides that, he wasn't quite sure how she would take it. It was too soon, he thought. They had become good friends, and he didn't want to spoil that. The time would come. He was sure. He found himself wishing that he could read her mind. What, exactly, was she thinking of him? Did she want what he wanted? He didn't want to rush things, but on the other hand, he didn't want to wait too long, didn't want her to think that something was wrong with him and get tired of waiting.

"I guess we ought to go back to the Spalding House and clean up. Get a bite to eat," he said. "You'll have to be at work soon."

"Yeah," she said. "I guess so."

They started out the door almost together, and their shoulders touched. Tod started to back off.

"Excuse me," he said, but she turned to face him, and she reached forward and took hold of his arms with her hands. She stepped in close and pulled him to her. Her face was turned up, and there was something in her eyes. Something . . . Tod felt his knees weaken. He lowered his face to meet hers, and his lips brushed hers. He felt lightheaded. Her hand went behind his head and pulled, and she pressed her lips hard against his. She kissed him hungrily, and he responded. Finally, she stepped back.

"I hope you don't think I'm too forward," she said.

"I think you're wonderful," said Tod. He kissed her again. "When this house is ready . . ."

"What?"

"I—I know we haven't known each other very long," he said. "Maybe it's too soon."

"Too soon for what?"

"When the house is ready, will you move into it with me? I mean, will you let it be *our* house? Will you marry me?"

"Of course I will," she said, and she kissed him again. "We'd better go now."

Clarence Dodd was beginning to feel sick. Every step the horse took made him reel. He thought that he would not be able to stay in the saddle much longer.

"We've gone the whole length of this damned road," said Vernon Bancroft. "You ain't seen nothing you remember. Damn it, boy, I hope you ain't funning with me."

"No sir," said Clarence. "I just can't think straight. I'm sick. I feel dizzy, and my head's hot. I—I think I might faint."

Bancroft rode up close to Clarence and reached a hand over to feel the young man's forehead.

"Damn," he said. "He ain't lying. He's burning up with fever."

"He ain't never going to find that gold for us," said Truitt.

"Shut up," said Bancroft. "Are you going to find that gold for us, boy? Are you?"

"I . . ."

Clarence reeled and pitched sideways almost out of the saddle, but the old man caught him. He was unconscious.

"Lon," said Bancroft, "you boys get him back to the shack and put him back to bed. Hurry it up."

Truitt and Carter moved in to take the unconscious Clarence from Bancroft.

"You get off your horse and get up behind him to hold him on," said Bancroft. "And be gentle with him. No rough stuff. You hear me? He's our ticket to gold. I'll fix up some stuff to doctor him some more. Now get going."

Truitt climbed up behind Clarence and turned the horse toward the Hard Biscuit. Carter followed. Bancroft got down off his horse and looked off the side of the road at the trees that were growing there. He found what he wanted and started walking toward it, reaching into a pocket at the same time and withdrawing a penknife.

When Truitt, holding Clarence in front of him, and Carter, leading Truitt's horse, arrived back at the Hard Biscuit, they were met by Hartley, who had been left alone to watch the place. Hartley walked out to meet the riders.

"What the hell's the matter with him?" he asked.

"Aw," said Truitt, "he's playing sick. Get him down off of here for me, will you?"

Hartley dragged Clarence out of the saddle, and

Truitt slipped off over the horse's rump.

"Take care of the horses, Irv," he said. He grabbed Clarence by the legs; Hartley already had him by the arms. They carried him into the shack and over to the cot, onto which they pitched him.

"Where's Vern?" asked Hartley.

"Gathering herbs, I guess," said Truitt. "He said something about doctoring this bastard."

He reached down and took hold of Clarence's shirt front, pulling his head up off the cot.

"Wake up," he said. "I know you're faking. Wake up."

He slapped Clarence across the face. Clarence did not react, and he slapped him again. Just then the door opened and Bancroft, his hands full of pieces of bark and various roots, stepped in. Bancroft stared at Truitt for a moment in disbelief, then put aside his harvest. Truitt lowered Clarence's head back down on the cot and straightened up. He looked at Bancroft.

"Vern," he said, "I—"

"Shut up," said Bancroft, taking two long strides across the room toward Truitt. "Didn't I say to be gentle?"

He grabbed Truitt by his shirt and spun him around. Then he swung his big right fist and smashed it into the side of Truitt's jaw, sending him across the room and into the far wall. Before Truitt could recover, Bancroft had him again. This time he jerked him up by the shirt front and bashed him into the wall head first, once, twice.

"Open the damn door!" he shouted.

Hartley rushed to the door and opened it, and

Bancroft dragged Truitt across the room and flung him headlong out into the yard. Still unsaddling horses outside, Carter watched bewildered as Truitt plowed up ground with his jaw. Bancroft turned back to his business.

"Boil me up some fresh water," he said, "and be quick."

Hartley grabbed a bucket and ran outside to do as he had been told, while Bancroft dragged a chair up close to the cot. He put a hand on Clarence's forehead.

"It's going to be all right, boy," he said. "I'll have you feeling better in no time. Then you'll find the gold for us, and everything will be all right. You bet. Everything's going to be all right."

Outside, Carter had walked over to where Truitt was getting shakily to his feet. His nose was bleeding from having been bashed against the wall, and one side of his face was raw from scraping dirt.

"What the hell was that all about?" asked Carter.

"One of these days," said Truitt, "I'm going to kill that old son of a bitch."

"There's no time like the present," said Carter. "That's what my mama used to say."

"My face hurts too bad right now," said Truitt. "I'll kill him later."

Matt rode up toward the mines. This northern mining country was sure different from Texas, he thought. Kyle was up in this part of the country, working the gold fields. Matt was getting a good taste of what gold could do to human beings, and he didn't envy Kyle his chosen environment.

He jerked his mind back to the present. He didn't
need to be thinking about other things. He had rid-
den up this mountain road with a purpose. He was
looking for someone or for evidence of that someone. Off to his left, he saw an old abandoned mine.
He nudged the black in that direction. There were
no tracks around the mine shaft entrance or anywhere near the old shack. It looked as if no one had
been on the property for years. Just the same, Matt
rode around the shack and up to the mine entrance.
He dismounted and walked a few steps into the mine.
Then he walked over to the shack and opened the
door. It creaked on its rusty old hinges, and he
stepped inside. The rude furniture was still there,
covered with dust. Matt went back outside and
climbed up on the stallion's back.

"Come on," he said.

He rode back out onto the road and continued on
his way. He passed by and checked out three more
such abandoned mines before he saw the Hard Biscuit. It looked much like the others, the same run-
down condition, except that smoke came out the
chimney of the shack and there were saddled horses
in a small corral. There were also lots of fresh tracks,
and as Matt drew closer, he could see two men out
in the yard. He turned the black toward them. One
of the two men pulled a six-gun out of its holster,
while the other trotted over to the shack to pick up
a rifle that was leaning against it. Then they stood
side by side and waited for Matt to draw nearer.

"That's far enough, mister," said Carter.

"Howdy," said Matt. "Name's Matt Ramsey."

"What the hell you doing here?" asked Carter.

Truitt stood with his six-gun in hand and his face partially diverted from Matt's view. He said nothing.

"Just riding by. I saw your smoke. Thought you might spare a cup of coffee."

"We ain't got no coffee," said Carter.

Matt started to swing his leg over the black to dismount.

"Well then," he said, "just a drink of water."

"Stay on that horse, mister," said Carter.

Matt swung back into his saddle. He stared at Carter and then at Truitt. He glanced over at the shack. Hartley was peeking out a window, and Matt could see the face. He held his hands out to his sides in a nonthreatening gesture.

"All right," he said. "Hell, I was just looking for a little hospitality, that's all."

"Well," said Carter, "you ain't going to find none of that here. You just move on back there out in the road and get on down the mountain."

"I'm going," said Matt. He backed the stallion toward the road. "Be seeing you."

As Matt reached the road and turned his horse to head back down toward Lane Rock, Carter shouted after him.

"You better hope not, mister," he yelled. "You might get dead!"

CHAPTER

★ 13 ★

Matt rode back into Lane Rock and stopped in front
of the marshal's office. He had argued with himself
all the way down the mountain. Stilwell had already
said that he was no longer interested in the possible
kidnaping of the impostor. He had been emphatic
about it. Yet Matt decided that he should give the
law one more chance. He tied the black to the hitching rail and went into Stilwell's office. The marshal
was there behind his desk.

"Hello, Ramsey," he said. "I didn't expect to see
you back in here."

"I didn't expect to be here," said Matt. "I just
took a ride up the mountain. I came across the Hard
Biscuit Mine. Two men in the yard. Another in the
shack. Maybe more."

"Any sign of Vernon Bancroft?" said Stilwell.
"He's been digging gold out of that mine for years."

"Yeah, well, maybe the men I saw think they're going to get their hands on some gold by some other means."

"What are you talking about?" asked the marshal.

"I rode up into the yard," said Matt. "They pulled guns on me. Told me to get the hell out of there."

"That don't mean nothing, Ramsey," said Stilwell. "They're about the unfriendliest bunch of folks around these parts."

"That may be," said Matt, "but I got a real strong feeling that they had a reason for not wanting me near that shack. Like maybe there's something—or somebody—in there that they didn't want me to see. And that ain't all. Glen told me this morning that two of that bunch left the bar for a while the night that boy disappeared. They were gone when he went out, and they came back in later."

"He didn't tell me that," said Stilwell.

"He told me."

"Come on," said Stilwell. "Let's go see Glen."

They walked together without speaking down the street to the Spalding House. Inside, they found Glen behind the bar.

"Glen," asked Stilwell, "the night that fake Stover left out of here, who was in the bar?"

"Bancroft and his boys," said Glen, "like I told you before. Only thing, Hartley and Truitt left for a while. A little bit before the kid went out back. They come back later and stayed until I closed the place."

"Why didn't you tell me that before?" asked Stilwell.

"I didn't think of it. Didn't remember. Ramsey

here came in and started asking me about it again, and it come back to me."

"Damn," said Stilwell. "We sure got a bunch of faulty memories around this town all of a sudden."

"Stilwell," said Matt, "he's up there at the Hard Biscuit. They still think he's Stover, and they're trying to make him tell them where the gold is. If he's smart, he'll string them along the same way he was doing you folks. He'll pretend to be trying to remember. If they find out he's an impostor, they'll kill him. If they decide that he just ain't going to remember, if they get tired of waiting, they'll kill him anyway. They might kill him accidentally just trying to beat the information out of him. Any way you look at it, that boy's life is in danger."

"He brought it on himself," said Stilwell.

"I'm talking about preventing a murder, Stilwell."

"You haven't presented me with any evidence of a crime. I'm not going up there and barging in on Bancroft just on your suspicions. Stop back in and see me again some time, Ramsey. But don't expect me to go running off with you unless you've got some hard evidence."

Stilwell turned and walked out of the Spalding House. Matt leaned on the bar. He doubled up a fist and bounced it off the bar a couple of times.

"Damn," he said.

"He ain't going to do anything, is he?" said Glen.

"Nope," said Matt.

"You want a drink?"

"Whiskey," said Matt.

Glen set a glass in front of Matt and poured it full from a bottle.

"It's on me," he said.

Matt finished the drink and walked over to the hotel desk. Spalding was there.

"Figure up my bill," said Matt. "I want to pay it off and check out."

"You leaving us, Mr. Ramsey?" asked Spalding.

"I just can't afford any more of this high living," said Matt. "I'll camp out somewhere outside of town."

"Well, Mr. Ramsey, your room and board was promised to you when you moved in."

"That was just because I was with the man you all thought was Tod Stover. Turns out he wasn't Stover. I ain't holding you or the town to that promise. Figure it up, Mr. Spalding."

Spalding did some quick figuring and came up with a total. He turned the bill around to face Matt.

"Is the, uh, fake Tod Stover's bill much more than that?" asked Matt.

"Well," said Spalding, "there are a few more drinks on his bill. Let me see here."

He did some more figuring and showed Matt another total.

"I'll pay it," said Matt.

"All of it? I mean, both bills?"

"Both bills."

Matt laid out his money on the counter while Spalding marked both bills paid in full.

"I sure do appreciate this, Mr. Ramsey," said Spalding. "You sure didn't have to do it."

Matt was halfway to the door when he had an afterthought. He turned back toward Spalding.

"Say," he said, "all those abandoned mines up the mountain road . . ."

"Yeah?"

"Would it bother anyone if I camped out in one of those shacks for a spell?"

"Why, no," said Spalding. "Help yourself. They're pretty run-down. Dirty."

"Yeah," said Matt. "I looked into a few of them today. Thanks."

Vernon Bancroft was seated beside the cot. He wrung the excess water out of a rag into a bowl of water that was sitting on the floor beside his chair. Then he carefully folded the rag and began to bathe the hot forehead of Clarence Dodd.

"There," he said. "Is that any better?"

"Yes," said Clarence.

"That tea I made for you ought to start taking effect," said the old man. "And the gunshot wound is looking a whole lot better. You're going to be all right."

"When can he ride again?" asked Carter, who was standing against the wall and watching.

"There ain't no hurry for that," said Bancroft. "He's got to get well first. That gold has waited for ten years. It can wait a few more days."

Carter left the shack and found Truitt out in the yard. Truitt's scraped face had begun to scab over.

"What's going on?" asked Truitt.

"Aw," said Carter, "Vern's in there daubing at the kid's face with a wet rag."

"He's taken a liking to that little snot," said Truitt. "We don't watch out, Vern's going to double-cross

Will McLennan

us. He's going to let that boy go free. You seen what
he done to me, and all I done was just to slap the
little shit a little. That's all. And look at my face.
He likes him better than us, Irv."

Irvin Carter shoved dirt around with the toe of his
boot. His hands were in his hip pockets.

"He just now told me that there weren't no hurry
for us to go after that gold," he said.

"See?" said Truitt. "That's what I mean. He was
in an all-fired hurry couple of days ago. Now there
ain't no hurry."

"Lon," said Carter, "let's take off. Let's just ride
out of here and leave the old son of a bitch with his
new pet. He don't like us no more. He don't want
us around nohow."

"We can't do that," said Truitt. "For one thing,
we ain't got no money. No place to go. There's all
that gold around here somewhere. We might as well
get it before we go. And besides all that, if we just
take off, one of these days we'll run across old Vern,
and he'll kill us deader'n hell."

"Well, what do we do then? Just lay around here
and do what he says while he pampers that boy in
there?"

"For now, Irv," said Truitt. "For now. But when
the time's right, I'm going to kill old Vern, and then
we can make that kid in there talk. I know how to
make him talk. We'll get rid of Vern, and then we'll
take the gold all for our own selves."

Carter kicked some more dirt around. He looked
up once at Truitt, who was standing with the scabby
side of his face turned away from Carter's line of
vision.

"Lon?" he said.

"Yeah."

"What about Mel? Will he go along with us?"

"I don't know. We'll just have to ask him, but we'll have to be careful how we do it. Let me ask him. I'll just kind of feel him out. See where he stands."

"What if he won't go along?"

"Then we'll just have to kill him, too," said Truitt. "That's all. Kill him, too."

There was an abandoned mine a little farther up the mountain and on the other side of the road from the Hard Biscuit. Matt remembered it from his ride out there, and he thought that he could keep an eye on Bancroft's crew pretty well from up there. After having paid both his and Clarence's bills at the Spalding House, he was damn near broke. He still had some trail food, and as long as he had bullets, he knew that he could eat. He stopped by the general store in Lane Rock and spent the last of his money on extra ammunition. Then with his saddle roll once more strapped on behind the saddle, he rode again up the mountain. He was cautious in passing by the Hard Biscuit, and he thought that he had made it all right without being seen. In a little while after that, he had arrived at his destination.

The trail that led off the road was steep and winding but by no means impassable. At the end of the trail a flat yard had been hacked into the side of the mountain. A small corral sat beside a shack at the back of the yard, the back wall of each being the mountain itself. On the side of the shack opposite

the corral, a footpath led to a mine shaft entrance.
Matt put the stallion in the small corral and picked
up the fallen rail to close it in. He pulled the saddle
and saddle roll off the horse's back and carried them
into the shack. Inside was a bunk built against one
wall, a table with two stools in the middle of the
room, and a woodstove. A shelf on one wall still held
a variety of dishes and bottles. A shallow pan, probably once used for panning gold, was hanging from
a peg on the wall, and a broom stood in one corner.
Matt put down his saddle and blanket roll and looked
around some more. With a little cleaning, it would
do. He stepped back outside. The high perch gave
him a commanding view of the Hard Biscuit Mine.
It also gave him a view of a small grove beside the
road below. There would be grazing for the black.
He decided to take the horse back down and stake
him out there. The small corral beside the shack had
been practically hacked from rock, and there was
nothing there for the animal to eat.

Clarence was feeling better, but he didn't want to
let on. The old man seemed to have softened up a
bit. He wasn't pressuring Clarence anymore about
getting out to find the gold. Clarence figured he could
play the invalid a little longer and thereby delay any
action. The three younger men lacked the patience
of the old one, and he was a little worried about
them, but so far, the old man seemed to be pretty
much in control. Clarence was dreadfully afraid,
though. Sooner or later his captors were bound to
tire of the waiting game. They would find out the
truth—that he did not know where any gold was

hidden, that he was not Tod Stover. Then they would kill him. He didn't know what he would do when that time came. He had tried once to make a break for it, and he had gotten himself shot for his trouble. He would just have to wait and see. He would postpone the inevitable as long as he could.

He wondered where Matt Ramsey was. At times he fantasized about Matt bursting in the door and blazing away with his big Colt to rescue him from his tormentors. But then he would think more realistically. Matt didn't know where to find him, and even if he did, he probably wouldn't bother. After all, he had lied to Matt, too, deceived him as he had deceived all the others. But maybe they didn't know yet. Maybe the whole town would come out to rescue Tod Stover, the hoped-for savior of Lane Rock.

It was late. Tod Stover had taken a long walk with Rosalie after she had gotten off work, and he had kissed her good night at her hotel-room door. It had been a long and lingering kiss, one that promised much more later, and Tod had gone on to his own room with a light and airy head. In his room he unbuttoned and pulled off one shoe. Then he sat, holding the shoe in his hand. Something wasn't right. He had a restless feeling about him. Was it just his longing for Rosalie? No. It was something more than that. He put the shoe back on and buttoned it up again. Then he left the room and locked the door behind him. He walked downstairs and out into the street. The sky was clear and the stars were bright overhead. He turned west and continued walking. As he walked along he thought to himself that never in Boston had he seen such stars, such a clear sky, such a night. The air was fresh and crisp and just a bit chilly. He walked until he found himself at his house. He and Rosalie had done a pretty good job of cleaning so far. Repairs and repainting and cleaning up the yard were all still to be done, but inside the house was at least clean. He went inside.

It was dark, but Tod knew his way. The strange feeling from the hotel room was still with him. He knew where he was going, what he was going to do, but he didn't know why he was doing it. It was as if something were driving him along. He went into the bedroom, his own old, childhood bedroom, and he took off his shoes and his coat and his vest and his shirt, and he stretched himself out on the old bed, and he closed his eyes.

CHAPTER
★ 14 ★

Tod might have slept. He couldn't be sure. All he knew was that time passed. The memory of his father coming into the room was vivid. It might have been a dream. But to Tod it was as if he were reliving that night ten years ago, a night he could never forget. His father came into the room and shook him by the shoulder.

"Tod," he said, "wake up."

Tod tried to open his eyes. It was dark. It was the middle of the night. He was half asleep, and he couldn't figure out what was going on. Was something wrong? Why was his father waking him up like this in the middle of the night?

"What's wrong?" he said.

"Everything's going to be all right," his father said, "but we have to hurry. Come on. Get up."

He didn't move fast enough. His father helped him

up—really pulled him up to a sitting position—then looked around for Tod's trousers.

"Here," he said, "put these on."

He remembered every detail of the dressing. He couldn't move fast enough to satisfy his father. The father pulled his clothes on him, tucked the shirt tail in, buttoned up the buttons. Tod was dressed, but he was still drowsy and befuddled. He still didn't know what was going on. He had a cold fear and a feeling of total helplessness. Something was happening to him, something was changing his life, and it was something totally beyond his control. His father seemed to be doing it, but something about his father told him that even that strong man was being moved by bigger events. There was an urgency in his father's voice and his movements that Tod had never seen or heard before. Was it fear he saw in his father that night? He couldn't imagine his father being afraid of anything. But something was very wrong.

Then it became obvious even to the ten-year-old Tod that his father had been planning this move. He grabbed a bag in which he had already packed Tod's clothes, and he grabbed Tod by the hand. He hurried him out into the dark night, and there in the road in front of the house a buggy stood waiting. A horse was hitched up to it, and it was ready to go. His father had been busy for some time, and Tod had not known, had not even been suspicious that anything was going on. He tried to climb up into the buggy, but once again, he was not fast enough. His father grabbed him from behind and helped him up. Then they were driving through the night, headed for the mountain road.

"Where are we going?" Tod shouted.

"I have to do something up there," his father said.

"Then we're leaving Lane Rock. We're moving."

"For good?" Tod asked.

"For good," his father answered.

Tod seemed to wake up, although he couldn't be sure that he had ever actually been asleep. He was standing in front of the house beside the road, and he was almost surprised that the horse and buggy were not standing there. He walked out into the middle of the road and turned to face west, and he looked to where the road began to wind itself up the mountainside. Then he was wide awake, and he knew that the answer was up that road.

Matt Ramsey slept that night on the ground just in front of the mining shack. The black stallion was down below. Matt had cooked his own meal on the stove inside, but he had taken it outside to eat. He had spent his time watching the Hard Biscuit below and down the road. He had seen Vernon Bancroft and his three men come and go, but he had seen nothing more significant. If they had a prisoner down there, they would probably keep him out of sight. In the mine shaft, perhaps. More likely in the shack. He had watched until well after dark, then he had spread his bedroll on the ground and gone to bed for the night. He was trying to figure out just what he should do. He couldn't just go down there and ask if those men were holding a prisoner. It would be unwise for one man to assault the mine. There were four hardcases down there. They were well armed and very unfriendly. He was hoping for more solid evidence of the presence down there of the man he had known as Tod Stover. That was his first goal: to know beyond a doubt that the man was there and was being held against his will. Once he knew that for sure, then he would worry more about the next step.

He slept not long but well enough. In a way it had been a relief to be out under the stars again and to feel the earth beneath his body rather than a feather bed. The night had been cool and crisp, and the air was fresh and clean. He was up before the sun, and he made himself some coffee. He took a cup of the hot, black liquid with him and found himself a comfortable seat from which to watch the movements at the Hard Biscuit. By the time the cup was empty, the sun had made its initial appearance on the far horizon. Soon smoke came from the chimney of the shack down below. The inhabitants of the Hard Biscuit were beginning to stir. Matt found his army field glasses and focused them on the shack.

One of the younger men stepped out the door in his long underwear and stretched. Matt did not know the three men by name. The only name he knew was Vernon Bancroft. The man scratched himself and walked around to the side of the shack, where he relieved his bladder. Then he went back inside. Matt put down the glasses and waited. He rolled himself a cigarette and smoked it, and then he got up to pour himself another cup of coffee. He sat back down to watch.

Tod Stover hardly slept that night. He was at the Spalding House before it was open for breakfast.

He wasn't really hungry. He was too excited to eat, but he did want some coffee to help him start his day. And he wanted to see Rosalie. Rosalie had to share this day with him. Spalding was the first one to make an appearance, and Tod rushed up to him right away.

"Mr. Spalding," he said, his voice betraying his excitement, "I need to talk to you."

"Well, come on with me while I put on the coffee," said Spalding. "What is it?"

"I know where the gold is. I remembered it all last night. I slept over in my house. My old house, you know. I slept in my old bed in my old room, and it all came back to me. It was almost as if I were ten years old again, and I relived it all. It was—it was almost real!"

"Where is it?" asked Spalding.

"I can't tell you," said Tod. "But I know that I can go straight to it. I know I can."

"When can we go?"

"Right away," said Tod. "I've been up all night. I'm ready. Well, almost."

"What do you mean, almost?" said Spalding, a worried look coming across his face.

"Well, I want to know if Rosalie can take the day off," said Tod. "I'd like for her to come along. And I think that we should talk to Mr. Hubbard. Don't you? He might like to come along. And the other council members? What do you think?"

"I think you're right. Just let me get this coffee started. We'll all need some coffee before we start out, I think. I'll get it started, and I'll round up the mayor and the council."

"And Rosalie?" asked Tod.

"Oh. Yes. Of course, she'll go with us."

Clarence woke up to the smell of coffee in the mining shack. His shoulder still ached with a dull pain, but his head felt much better. He no longer felt sick. He opened his eyes, and there was Bancroft watching him, as if the old man had been waiting patiently for him to wake up.

"Well, boy," said Bancroft. "You're awake. How are you feeling this morning?"

"Much better," said Clarence, and as soon as he had said it, he felt like a fool. He should not have admitted the truth to the old man, he thought. He should have pretended to still feel sick. Perhaps he might have been able to prolong the inevitable another day. But it was too late. He had said it, and he couldn't take it back.

"Good," said Bancroft. "We'll have a little coffee and a bite to eat, and then we'll go out and ride again. Maybe you'll find it today. Maybe you'll remember since you're feeling better."

"I—I have to go out back," said Clarence.

"Here then. Let me help you up."

Bancroft gently helped Clarence up from the cot. Truitt scowled at the old man's mild manner from across the room. He shot a sideways glance at Carter, who raised his eyebrows and then looked quickly away.

"Come on," said Bancroft. "I'll go along with you. We can't have you trying anything foolish again. Don't want you to get hurt anymore. Come on."

• • •

Matt was watching from his perch up above when Clarence stepped out the door of the shack, followed closely by Bancroft. Matt sat up straight and squinted his eyes for a second, then he picked up the field glasses and sighted them on Clarence.

"It's him, all right," he said. "By God, I was right."

He had the answer to the question. Now he was faced with the next step: What to do? How could he get the young man safely away from his captors? He could go back to town and tell the marshal that he had actually seen him there at the Hard Biscuit, but that probably wouldn't budge Stilwell. Stilwell would just say, so what? Matt couldn't just haul out his guns and go running into the camp. There were four armed men down there. He couldn't fight them all by himself. Even if he could, it would put the young man in too much danger. He might get the very man he was trying to rescue killed instead of freed. For now, he decided, he would just keep watching.

At the Spalding House the coffee was made and poured. Tod Stover sat with Rosalie on one side and Spalding on the other. Emerson Hubbard was directly across the table from him, and Lester Wiggins sat next to the mayor. Harvel Beck and Eldon Gray were there, and Howard Box and Clell Harman were expected shortly.

"I know I can go right to it," said Tod. "Once we start up that road, I'll go right to it. The events of the whole night are alive in my mind."

"We're all excited about this, Mr. Stover," said Hubbard, "but try to calm down. Let's wait until everybody's here so you don't have to go over everything twice. When we're all together we can talk it all out."

"There's really nothing to talk about, Mr. Mayor," said Tod. "We'll just ride up there and get it. That's all there is to it. It's so simple. Now that it all came back to me, it's so easy. I knew it all before I was struck on the head. This is what I had planned to do in the first place. Then I was injured in Boston before I could catch my train, and I lost my memory for a while. It had all come back to me except the events of that night, and they came back last night in my house. It's so simple."

Rosalie put a hand on Tod's arm.

"It's wonderful, Tod," she said. "I'm so glad you're all better."

"What is it?" said Marshal Stilwell, just walking in the door. "We going after the gold?"

"Just hold on, Lloyd," said Hubbard. "I was just telling Mr. Stover here to wait until we're all together, and he can tell his story one time only and we can decide what to do."

"Who are we waiting for?" asked Stilwell.

"Howard Box and Clell Harman," said Wiggins.

"What do we need with them?" said Stilwell. "There's enough here to make a decision, ain't there?"

"Lloyd," said Hubbard, "get yourself a cup of coffee and sit down and shut up. We need the whole town council here. This is an important day for Lane Rock. Besides, we've waited ten years already. A few more minutes won't hurt us none."

"I'll get you some coffee," said Spalding. While

he was up pouring the coffee, the door opened and Box came in.

"Clell's coming," he said. "He's just down the street."

Spalding filled two more cups and set them on the table. By the time Box had sat down, Harman was coming in the door. At last, the mayor, the marshal, and the entire town council were present. Hubbard stood up.

"All right," he said. "We're all here. We'll get right to it. Mr. Stover has something to tell us."

"I think everyone already knows," said Tod. "There's not really much to tell. It all came back to me last night. I know where the gold is. At least, I know where my father hid it ten years ago. And I'm ready to lead you to it. Right now."

"Where is it?" asked Stilwell.

"I can't tell you," said Tod. "I have to go there. But I can go straight to it. I know I can."

"Well, is it in town?" asked Wiggins.

"No. It's outside of town. It's up the mountain road."

"We'll need horses," said Wiggins. "And a wagon for the gold. I can take care of that. Are we all going?"

"I think we should all go," said the mayor. "Are there any objections?"

There were none.

"All right," he said. "We're all going."

"Then I suggest," said Wiggins, "uh, may I, Mr. Mayor?"

"Please do, Lester," said Hubbard.

"I suggest that we adjourn, and those who have

their own horses can go get them. Those who need horses can come along with me to the stable. I'll drive the wagon. Let's all meet back here ready to go in, say, half an hour?"

Hubbard looked over the faces. No one made any response to Wiggins's proposal.

"Good," said Hubbard. "That's what it will be. If you need a mount, follow Lester. Be back here in front of the hotel in half an hour. Friends, this is a big day."

Everyone stood up to go, and as they did, Rosalie grabbed Tod with both arms and hugged him to her.

"I'm so proud of you!" she said.

"I'm glad you're here with me," said Tod, "to share this day."

"Well," she said, "we'd better run along with Mr. Wiggins. Neither one of us has a horse."

CHAPTER
★ 15 ★

Lane Rock had never before seen anything quite like it, not even in the early gold rush days. Lester Wiggins pulled up in front of the Spalding House driving a buckboard, and close behind him came Tod Stover and Rosalie Bancroft in a buggy. Stilwell and Spalding were waiting there for them on horseback. Glen stood on the sidewalk, looking lonely and left out.

"Hell, Glen," said Spalding, "lock the doors and come on along with us."

Glen wasted no time in following his boss's advice. He had no horse, so he climbed aboard the wagon with Wiggins. Hubbard showed up on the back of a prancing white donkey with an expensive, elaborately decorated saddle. His appearance was ludicrous, but the donkey was better behaved than most horses, and it stepped with pride. Hubbard sat haughtily in the saddle. Harvel Beck and Eldon Gray showed up on horseback, but Howard Box came in a buggy with his wife beside him, and Clell Harman was in a buckboard, also accompanied by his wife. The four Harman children rode in the back of the buckboard. But that wasn't the end of it. Others showed up on horseback and in buckboards and in buggies. Two members of Lane Rock's volunteer hose company showed up driving the jumper, or hose cart. Several stray dogs came into the street to join in the excitement, and these began barking and nipping around the fetlocks of the horses and Mayor Hubbard's donkey. One horse started to buck, which only made the dogs bark more. And the bucking horse banged into another horse, nearly unseating its rider. The street in front of the Spalding House—indeed, the street the whole length of town—became a scene of near-total chaos.

"God damn," said Hubbard. "The whole town's come out."

People were still coming from both ends of the street. The undertaker had even come in his hearse.

"Let's get going," Hubbard shouted to Stilwell.

"Where the hell are we going?" Stilwell shouted back.

"Hell, Lloyd, I don't know. Stover's the only one who knows."

"Then we'll have to follow Stover," said Stilwell.

"All right," said Hubbard. "Then get him started."

Stilwell snaked his way through the throng of men and beasts until he came up alongside the buggy in which Tod and Rosalie sat.

"Let's go, Stover," he said. "Lead on."

Tod looked at Stilwell with a blank expression on his face.

"Well," said the marshal, "what are you waiting for?"

Tod looked ahead, his expression now showing hopelessness. Stilwell followed his gaze. There was no way Tod could move his buggy. Riders on horseback and in wagons and buggies all crowded the street, from one side to the other.

"Damn!" said Stilwell. Then he started shouting orders and shoving people and animals this way and that. His actions seemed only to increase the confusion. He took a deep breath and was about to shout again when he heard a woman scream from somewhere behind him. With some difficulty, he got his horse turned around. Amazingly, amidst the teeming chaotic throng, he spied a small area of particularly intense disorder. He tried to ride over to it, but he couldn't get his horse through the crowded mass. He dismounted and shouldered and edged his way through to a wagon with a man and a woman on the seat, the woman having slid down on her spine, her legs extended out straight in front of her, her hands on her swollen belly and beads of sweat on her forehead. She moaned aloud, and the moan extended itself into a loud wail. The man was looking around in helpless panic. In the bed of the wagon were four small children, all watching the woman with wide eyes. People around the wagon were also watching in wonder.

"Get a doctor!" shouted the desperate man. "She's going to have it right here!"

"There ain't a doctor in fifty miles," said a man in the crowd.

"Well somebody do something!" shouted the man on the wagon seat.

Stilwell stretched his neck and looked around the crowd.

"Where's Aunt Maudie?" he called. "Maude Draper? Where are you?"

A husky woman of indeterminate age elbowed her way through the mob toward the wagon.

"Here I am," she said. "Get out of my way. Let me through. I'm a-coming. Hold your horses."

"Aunt Maudie's coming, Quince," said Stilwell. "Now you just tell Miz Brice to hold on."

"Ahh," shouted Mrs. Brice. "I can't hold on! I can't prevent it no longer."

Maude Draper made her way to the wagon by tossing one last man aside.

"Here I am, Lettie," she said. "Well, get her back in the bed. Don't you men know nothing? Lift her back there. Get them kids out of there. Move it!"

Stilwell clambered up onto the wagon seat with Lettie Brice and her husband. He hesitated a moment, then grabbed the moaning woman from behind, under her arms.

"Come on, Quince," he said.

Quincey Brice took hold of his wife's ankles, and he and Stilwell tried to lift her over the seat. She screamed. They groaned and struggled. Lettie Brice was a big woman, heavy even when she was not pregnant. Aunt Maudie found a man standing near and slapped him hard on the back.

"What are you standing here for?" she said. "Give them a hand!"

The man moved around the wagon and put his hands under Mrs. Brice's ample buttocks. The three men gave a concerted heave and carried her over the seat, but their combined strength didn't last long enough to let her down gently. She screamed again as she bounced on the wagon bed. The children were still there in the way, and Stilwell stepped on a boy's foot. The boy began to scream, but Maude reached up and slapped him across the back of the head.

"Get out of there!" she said. "That's what you get. All of you get out of there!"

The children, Brice, and Stilwell scattered in all directions, and Maudie climbed up into the wagon. Lettie's legs were spread wide. Maude knelt between her feet and took hold of the long, full skirt. Then she looked fiercely around her at the gawking crowd.

"What are you looking at?" she snapped. "Turn your heads. Get away from here!"

The children who had been chased from the wagon bed like so many cockroaches were hanging around the sides of the wagon, their eyes wide.

"Lloyd Stilwell," said Maude, "get these kids out of here. And make these men turn their heads."

"I don't know why they want to look," said Brice. "I'm about to get sick. I wisht I'd a gone fishing this morning like I meant to."

Lettie Brice screamed.

Matt Ramsey saw one of the men down at the Hard Biscuit begin to saddle the horses. Something was up down there. He strapped on his Colt, picked up his Winchester and his saddle, and headed down the mountain road. He found the black stallion grazing contentedly below, and he quickly saddled him up.

"Just be ready, old pard," he said. "We might need to go somewhere in a hurry."

Matt's view of the Hard Biscuit wasn't as good from the road level as it had been up at the abandoned mine site, but he was still on higher ground than they were. He walked out to the road and took a look. He could see where the path led off the road and into the Hard Biscuit. He wanted to see more. He inched his way down the road a ways until he found a spot from which he could see the front of the shack. Leaning back against a large rock on the side of the road, half shielded from their view, he settled back to watch.

"Are the horses ready to go?" asked Bancroft.

"Irv's getting them saddled," said Truitt.

"We got water?"

"Uh, I don't know."

"Well, find the canteens and get them filled," said Bancroft. "No telling how long we'll be out. Get a move on."

Truitt rummaged around the room until he located the canteens. He gathered them up and went outside. Bancroft turned on Hartley.

"What the hell are you doing?" he said.

"I'm just waiting here till we're ready to go," said Hartley.

"If everybody stands around and waits," said Bancroft, "we won't never be ready. Will we?"

"I guess not."

"Get out there and help Irv with the horses."

Hartley hurried out the door. Bancroft pulled on a shirt and stuffed its tail down into his trousers. Then he strapped on a six-gun. He turned to Clarence, who was still lying on the cot.

"You ready to get up, son?" he asked.

"I—I think so," said Clarence.

"Well, come on. I'll give you a hand."

The old man took Clarence gently by the arm and helped him sit up on the cot.

"Don't hurry it, now," he said.

Clarence put a hand to his head and feigned dizziness.

"I'll be all right," he said. "In a minute."

"All right," said Bancroft. "There ain't no hurry. You just take your time. Here."

He had picked up Clarence's jacket, and he threw it over the young man's shoulders and helped him get his arms into it. Clarence stood up.

"You going to make it all right?" asked Bancroft.

"Yeah," said Clarence. "I think so."

"Good," said Bancroft. "Good. Come on."

He took Clarence by the arm and walked outside with him as though he were escorting an invalid. The other three were already mounted up and waiting.

"Look at that," said Truitt. "It makes me sick."

"What are you going to do about it?" asked Carter.

"Wait and see."

Bancroft stepped up with Clarence and took a look at the horses. All five were saddled, but he saw something he didn't like.

"What the hell are you doing on that gray?" he said to Truitt.

"I'm fixing to ride her. What else?"

"Get down."

"Why? What's the difference what horse I ride?"

"This boy's a dude," said Bancroft, "and he's been sick. That gray's the gentlest horse we got, and you know it. Now get down."

Bancroft didn't wait for Truitt to obey. He reached up and grabbed Truitt by the back of his shirt and by the back of his belt and flung him from the saddle. Truitt landed with a thud on his left side. He rolled over on his back and reached for his six-gun, but he had it only halfway out of the holster when the old man's ancient Remington was leveled and cocked.

"Go on, boy," said Bancroft. "I'd just as soon scatter your brains as look at you. Go on. Go for it."

Truitt shoved his gun back into its holster and stared at Bancroft.

"Which horse do you want me to ride?" he asked.

"Get on that pinto," said Bancroft, and he turned to help Clarence up into the saddle on the back of the gray mare. "Come on," he said. "There you go. All right?"

"Yes sir," said Clarence. "I think so."

Truitt avoided the critical gaze of Carter as he climbed into the saddle of the pinto. Up the road, Matt Ramsey was aware of the activity at the Hard Biscuit. He chambered a shell into his Winchester and tried to decide what he was going to do. Should he let that bunch ride out with their prisoner, or should he start shooting? He wasn't sure. If he let them go, he would have to follow them, and he would have to try to do that without being seen. It would not be easy on this mountain road to keep them in sight and himself hidden at the same time. On the other hand, if he started shooting, he might easily endanger the very man he was trying to save. If he didn't make up his mind soon, he thought, they would be out in the road, and then it would be too late. He didn't want to start shooting. He had never been one to shoot first, never the one to start a fight. He had no stomach for unnecessary killing. He had left Texas to escape the memories of so much violence in his past.

"Damn," he said. He turned and ran back up the road to the spot where his black waited, already saddled, and he climbed up onto his back. He was off the road, hidden from the view of passersby in a little grove. He would wait and see in which direction they rode. He expected that it would be past him. There were only a couple of abandoned mine sites between the Hard Biscuit and Lane Rock. They had probably already examined those. He thought that they would be going up the mountain. He waited.

Bancroft was mounted up, and he rode up beside the gray mare on which Clarence sat.

"All right, son," he said. "Just relax. No one's rushing you. I want you to just ride along easy-like and look around. Something will trigger your recollections somewhere along the way. If it gets to be too much for you, let me know. There's always another day."

"Yes sir," said Clarence.

"But I got a feeling about today," said the old man. "Something's going to break today. I got a feeling."

He turned a hard gaze toward Truitt.

"Ride on out ahead," he said. "All three of you."

Truitt, a deep scowl on his face, urged his mount forward. Carter followed, then Hartley. Bancroft let them get ahead a distance before he shouted his next instruction.

"Turn up the mountain," he said.

Truitt was about to head up the mountain as he had been told when he suddenly pulled back hard on the reins.

"God damn!" he yelled.

"What's the matter?" shouted Bancroft.

"Something's a-coming up the hill," said Truitt.

CHAPTER
★ 16 ★

Truitt turned his horse so quickly that he ran into both Carter and Hartley. Hartley's mount reared and shrieked, tumbling its rider backward out of the saddle. Hartley yelled as he fell. He landed on his back with a dull thud, which knocked all the wind out of his lungs. Carter's horse began backing up, and Truitt's fidgeted. Behind them, Bancroft halted both his own and Clarence's mounts.

"What is it?" he shouted. "Who's coming?"

Up the road, Matt heard the noise. He spurred the black and headed downhill for the Hard Biscuit. Something was happening down there. He didn't know what it was, but he would find out.

The racket on down the road was being caused by the mob from Lane Rock. Miraculously, Stilwell had gotten Tod Stover's buggy in the lead, and now Tod was driving the buggy up the mountain road, followed by nearly the entire population of Lane Rock. It sounded like a troop of cavalry was approaching, except that a troop of cavalry would have had more discipline. In addition to the sound of many horses' hooves, there were loud and raucous voices and the clatter of numerous wagons and buggies. Tod was driving at an easy pace, looking to both sides of the road as he made his way up the mountain. When he came in view of the entrance to the Hard Biscuit, he slowed. Then he stopped. He looked, and he remembered. He looked into the excited face of Rosalie, sitting there beside him. He looked back toward the Hard Biscuit, and he pointed.

"It's there," he said.

Mayor Hubbard was riding his donkey just on the right of the buggy, and Lloyd Stilwell was riding alongside on the left.

"The Hard Biscuit?" asked the mayor.

"Oh, no," said Stilwell.

A rider just to the rear of the buggy had overheard, and he gave a loud whoop and spurred his horse, racing around the buggy and the mayor and heading hell for leather toward the entrance of the Hard Biscuit. A few others followed. Hartley was still on the ground, but he had just about gotten his breath back. His eyes opened wide as he saw the riders racing toward him. He jerked out his six-gun and fired a wild shot in their general direction.

"God damn!" he shouted. "Here they come."

He scampered to his feet and, forgetting his nervous horse, ran back toward the shack. The riders in the road, reacting to Hartley's shot, tried to turn their horses all at once. They ran into each other, one rider falling from his horse, another horse and rider both going down. The third managed to get turned around, and he raced back to rejoin the crowd.

"Lloyd," he said incredulously, "someone's shooting at us!"

"You damn fool," said Stilwell, "that's Bancroft's place."

The other two downed men ran on foot back to the safety of the crowd. Then Matt Ramsey came riding down. He stopped beside the buggy with Tod and Rosalie in it, and he looked at Stilwell.

"What the hell is all this?" he asked.

"We came for the gold," said Stilwell. "It was supposed to be just the town officials, but the word leaked out somehow, and the whole damn town followed us out here."

Matt looked at Tod. "You remembered?" he asked.

Tod pointed to the entrance of the Hard Biscuit.

"It's right in there," he said. "At least that's where Dad put it ten years ago."

"What are you doing here, Ramsey?" asked Stilwell.

"I've been watching that Bancroft bunch since you wouldn't do anything. They're the kidnapers, all right. They've got him in there. I've seen him."

"So that's why they shot at us," said Stilwell. "No way they're going to let us in there."

"I took a quick look as I rode past," said Matt. "They've all gone back into their holes, either in the shack or in the mine. Look, Stilwell, get this circus out of here before some of them get killed."

"A good idea, Lloyd," yelled Hubbard from the other side of the buggy. "Get them all back to town."

Stilwell turned his horse around to face the crowd behind him. He stood up in the stirrups and stretched his neck.

"All right, folks," he shouted. "Everyone turn around and head back down into town. There's been some shooting up here, and there's liable to be more. Go on now. Turn around. Get on back down."

Everyone tried to turn at once. Wagons and buggies with just enough room on the road to turn got in the way of the men on horseback. Some bold riders went down into the ditch on the north side of the road to get past the congestion. A wagon went off into the ditch and lost a wheel. People shouted and cursed at each other.

"You'd better go too," Matt said to Tod and Rosalie.

"I'm staying," said Tod. "Now that I know where that gold is, I'm not going anywhere until it's back where it belongs."

"I'm staying with Tod," said Rosalie. "Besides, that's my daddy in there."

"Well then," said Matt, "get down out of that buggy and get over there in the ditch."

"I believe I'll see all the people safely back to town," said Hubbard, turning his donkey.

"That's probably a good idea, Mr. Mayor," said Matt. With the crowd backed down the hill a safe distance, Matt ran over to join Tod and Rosalie in the ditch. There they had a good view of both the front of the shack and the mine entrance.

"Are you sure they're in there?" asked Tod. "I don't see any sign of life."

"They're in there," said Matt.

Lloyd Stilwell came back and jumped down into the ditch with them.

"See anything?" he asked.

"Nope," said Matt. "They're waiting for us to make the first move, I reckon."

"Damn," said Stilwell. "You got any ideas?"

"Ask them to surrender," said Matt.

"Sure," said Stilwell. "Why didn't I think of that?"

He stood up cautiously, looking toward the shack.

"Bancroft," he shouted. "Vernon Bancroft. Can you hear me?"

"I hear you," came Bancroft's voice.

"This is Lloyd Stilwell, Vern. Come on out and give yourself up. You ain't killed nobody. You ain't stole nothing. Don't make it any worse. Come on out and we won't shoot."

"You going to arrest us for nabbing Stover?" asked Bancroft.

"I don't know," said Stilwell. "Might be we'll work something out. That ain't even Stover you got in there."

"Damn it, Stilwell," said Matt. "What'd you have to tell them that for?"

Inside the shack, Truitt turned wild-eyed on Clarence. His revolver was already in his hand. Now he pointed it at Clarence and thumbed back the hammer.

"Not even Stover," he said. "And him getting pampered like a baby."

Bancroft stepped quickly between Clarence and

Truitt. His six-gun was aimed at Truitt's chest.

"Hold it, Lon," he said. "I don't know who he is, but we ain't going to kill him. We stop now, we might get out of this clean."

"But with no gold," said Truitt.

"Put your gun down," said Bancroft.

Truitt lowered his six-gun, and Bancroft turned to Clarence. He reached out with his left hand and took Clarence by the arm.

"Come on," he said. "We're going out."

Bancroft led Clarence across the room and opened the door.

"Go on," he said.

Clarence stepped outside. Bancroft was about to follow him, when Truitt suddenly raised his six-gun again and fired. The bullet struck Bancroft between the shoulder blades. The old man roared in pain and anger as Clarence ran for the road.

Matt stood up in the ditch. "Come on, boy!" he shouted.

Bancroft fell forward on the hard ground before the shack.

"Daddy!" screamed Rosalie. She tried to run toward her fallen father, but Tod held her down in the ditch. Matt and Stilwell both began firing at the open cabin door to keep anyone inside from shooting at the fleeing Clarence. Clarence made it to the ditch and jumped in.

"I'm glad to see you," he said to Matt.

"Soon as we get through here," said Matt, "I'm going to kick your butt. By the way, what the hell's your name?"

"I'm Clarence Dodd. I'm sorry I lied to you."

From inside the shack, someone started shooting through the front window. Stilwell fired a round through the window, and the shooter inside backed away.

"I'll give you one more chance," called Stilwell. "Come out with your hands up, and we won't shoot."

Truitt popped up in the window and fired a quick shot.

"Go to hell!" he yelled.

"We're getting nowhere like this," said Stilwell.

"Look!" said Matt.

Bancroft had rolled over onto his side, and now he began pushing himself along the ground with his feet. He was inching toward the shack—not the door, but the front wall to the uphill side of the door. With his right hand he was feeling inside his breast pocket.

"What's he doing?" said Stilwell.

"I don't know," said Matt.

Bancroft had gotten himself up close to the wall, and he pulled something out of his pocket. Then he reached under the shack and scraped up a pile of trash, loose twigs, and brush and such. He reached over with his right hand and made a scratching motion against the side of the shack.

"Matches," said Stilwell.

"He's going to burn them out," said Matt. "Get ready."

"Rosalie," asked Stilwell, "is there a back way out of that place?"

"The only way out is the front door," she said.

The flames grew quickly and licked greedily at the dry old boards on the shack. Inside, Truitt sniffed.

"What the hell's that?" he said.

"Smoke," said Carter. "They're burning us out!"

"I ain't going to burn," said Hartley. "I'm getting out of here!"

"Come on!" said Carter. He ran out the front door, followed closely by Hartley, and they fired toward the ditch as they ran. Stilwell fired back with his revolver. His first shot went wide, but his second hit Hartley in the stomach. Hartley dropped his gun and clutched at the gaping hole in his middle. He staggered backward until he bumped into the burning shack, then he dropped to his knees and slumped forward. The back of his shirt had caught fire. Carter was running and firing at the same time. His shots were all going wild. Matt took aim with his Winchester, but he didn't shoot. It didn't seem right. This man was shooting so wildly that he was really no threat. Carter got close to the mine entrance just as Stilwell shot him in the back. He ran three more steps and pitched forward, landing on his face just at the entrance to the tunnel. Stilwell started to stand up.

"There's another one in there," said Matt.

"Lon Truitt," said Rosalie. "He's the worst one of all."

"Truitt!" shouted Stilwell. "Come out of there! You don't want to burn to death."

There was no answer. The flames leaped higher. Soon the entire shack was enveloped in a roaring blaze. Rosalie turned her face away and buried it against Tod's chest.

"Damn," said Stilwell.

They heard no screams, just the crackling of the

flames as they consumed the weathered timbers of the shack. It didn't take long. The shack caved in, and the fire soon burned itself out. Matt and Stilwell stood up cautiously and walked slowly to the pile of ashes. Tod and Rosalie followed at some distance. The ash heap was too hot to rummage in, so they just walked around it and looked from the edges. They saw nothing that might have been Truitt. Matt did see an old ax and a couple of barely charred boards on the ground behind where the shack had been. He wondered about them, but he said nothing. Rosalie and Tod had stopped by the body of Vernon Bancroft. Both were on their knees. Rosalie was weeping silently, and Tod had an arm around her shoulders. Clarence approached and looked down at the old man.

"Is he . . ."

"He's dead," said Tod.

"Well," said Stilwell, "let's get that gold—if it's still here. That's what we came for."

Tod stood up and walked over to the mine entrance. Rosalie walked beside him, closely followed by Clarence and Stilwell. Matt held back. They stood for a moment at the dark hole in the side of the mountain, then Tod stepped inside. The walls of the tunnel had been boarded up like the inside walls of a house. Tod pointed to the bottom of the wall just to his left, just inside the entrance.

"There," he said.

Stilwell looked around and found an old pick on the ground. He took it up and began to pry at the boards. Soon he had two of them out, and there it was. Six bags.

"By God," he said. "It's really here!"

They carried the bags to the buggy and loaded it up.

"Let's get this stuff to town," said Stilwell. "I'll send someone out to take care of the bodies."

Rosalie looked back toward where her father lay.

"I hate to just leave him like that," she said.

"It'll be all right," said Tod. "It won't be for long."

Stilwell looked around.

"Hey," he said, "where the hell is Ramsey?"

"He was just here," said Tod.

"Damn," said Stilwell. "Well, come on. Let's get on down the mountain while we can."

Tod drove the buggy with the gold in it, with Rosalie at his side. They were accompanied by Stilwell riding a horse on one side and Clarence riding on the other side. They had not gone far when Lon Truitt stepped out from behind a boulder on the side of the road. He held a Henry repeating rifle in his hands. He worked the lever, chambering a shell, and with a deadly sneer on his face, he raised the rifle to his shoulder. He took careful aim at the middle of Stilwell's back. With the marshal down, the two dudes would be no problem. That would leave the gold and the girl for him. He didn't know what had become of the other man. He was gone, and that was enough. He was about to squeeze the trigger when he heard a voice behind him.

"Put it down."

He whirled and fired, but his shot went wide. Matt Ramsey's first shot from his Winchester smashed Truitt's left shoulder. Truitt made a noise like a hurt wild animal. His left arm hung useless at his side, but he raised the Henry with his right. Matt fired again. The bullet struck Truitt in the chest, causing his whole body to jerk. The right arm went limp, and the Henry fell to the ground. Truitt swayed backward, forward, from side to side. He died on his feet, and then the body crumpled up in a pile there in the middle of the mountain road.

When Matt got down to Lane Rock, he saw the buggy parked in front of Stilwell's office. He rode over there and tied the black stallion to the hitching rail. Then he went inside.

"Where the hell have you been, Ramsey?" asked Stilwell.

"I waited around for Truitt," he said. "I thought he'd show up again. He did."

"What happened?"

"He'll show up no more," said Matt.

Mayor Hubbard came into the office.

"Where is it?" he asked.

Stilwell pointed to a pile of sacks in a corner of his office, and Hubbard ran over to examine them.

"What's going to happen to me?" asked Clarence.

"I'm holding you," said Stilwell.

"On what charge?" asked Matt.

"Well," said Stilwell, "for starters, defrauding the town."

"You talking about that hotel bill?" asked Matt.

"Yeah."

"It's paid. Ask Spalding."

"You paid that?" said Clarence.

"Yeah," said Matt. "Any other charges, Stilwell?"

The marshal sighed loudly. "I guess not," he said. "You can go, Dodd."

"What're you going to do, boy?" asked Matt.

"I'm going back to Boston," said Clarence. "I'm going to the police to tell them what I did. If they ever let me out of jail, I'm going back to my father and try to make things up to him. I'd like to find a job here, though, long enough to earn my fare back home."

Tod Stover stepped up in front of Clarence. He stood for a moment looking him in the eye.

"I need some help on my house," he said. "Probably just about enough to earn you the price of that ticket."

"And what about you, Ramsey?" Stilwell asked. "What are you going to do?"

"I'm riding on west," said Matt. "Right now."

He got to the edge of Lane Rock and he stopped the black. He turned in the saddle and looked back at the town one last time. Then he turned back and reached down and patted the black.

"I knew that boy would turn out all right," Matt said, "if I could just keep him alive long enough. Let's go, big fellow."